SESAME STREET

Elmo and Zoe Fly a Kite

Wind comes and goes!
Be patient, it will be windy again. Bye!
What if we make our own wind? Let's blow on our kites!
You help blow, too!

MAKING THE MOST OF JR. CINE-MANGA®

Books use lots of creative techniques to tell stories. The speech balloons and sound effects in comic-style stories are an exciting way for your child to experience the printed word. Here's how you can make the experience even more interactive and playful:

- The first pages introduce the characters and the story. Point to the portraits as you name Elmo and his friends. When you revisit the book, ask your child to tell you who everyone is as you point to their labels and ask what they think the story will be about.

- As you read aloud, point to the words in the speech balloons and other words on the page. As you return to the stories, you'll find that kids will "read" some of the words along with you, especially the sound effects. Pages should be read from top to bottom, first the left-hand page, then the right.

- Change your voice from char ... ve to match Elmo's funny tones exactly...kids ... voices you put on.

- Cine-Manga uses dynamic ph ... mimic the actions they see the characters performing: tossing the kite up, huffing and puffing, putting on a thinking pose.

The look of comic books may be different from other picture books, but your child can learn and grow with them the same way they do with other stories. Visual storytelling can motivate children to communicate with pictures and the written word—the best of both worlds!

Contributing Editor - Tara Twedt
Graphic Designers and Letterers - Louis Csontos and John Lo
Cover Designers - Anne Marie Horne, Anna Kerbaum and Tomás Montalvo-Lagos

Digital Imaging Manager - Chris Buford
Production Managers - Jennifer Miller and Mutsumi Miyazaki
Senior Designer - Anna Kernbaum
Art Director - Matt Alford
Senior Editor - Elizabeth Hurchalla
Managing Editor - Jill Freshney
VP of Production - Ron Klamert
Editor in Chief - Mike Kiley
President & C.O.O. - John Parker
Publisher & C.E.O. - Stuart Levy

Written by MOLLY BOYLAN
Starring The Muppets™ of Sesame Street
KEVIN CLASH
FRAN BRILL
JOEY MAZZARINO
Also Featuring
DESIREE CASADO
ALAN E. MURAOKA

E-mail: info@TOKYOPOP.com
Come visit us online at www.TOKYOPOP.com

A Cine-Manga® Book
TOKYOPOP Inc.
5900 Wilshire Blvd., Suite 2000
Los Angeles, CA 90036

sesameworkshop™

The nonprofit educational organization
behind Sesame Street and so much more
www.sesameworkshop.org

Sesame Street: Elmo and Zoe Fly a Kite!

ISBN: 1-59532-746-0

First TOKYOPOP® printing: July 2005

10 9 8 7 6 5 4 3 2

Printed in the USA

SESAME STREET

Elmo and Zoe Fly a Kite

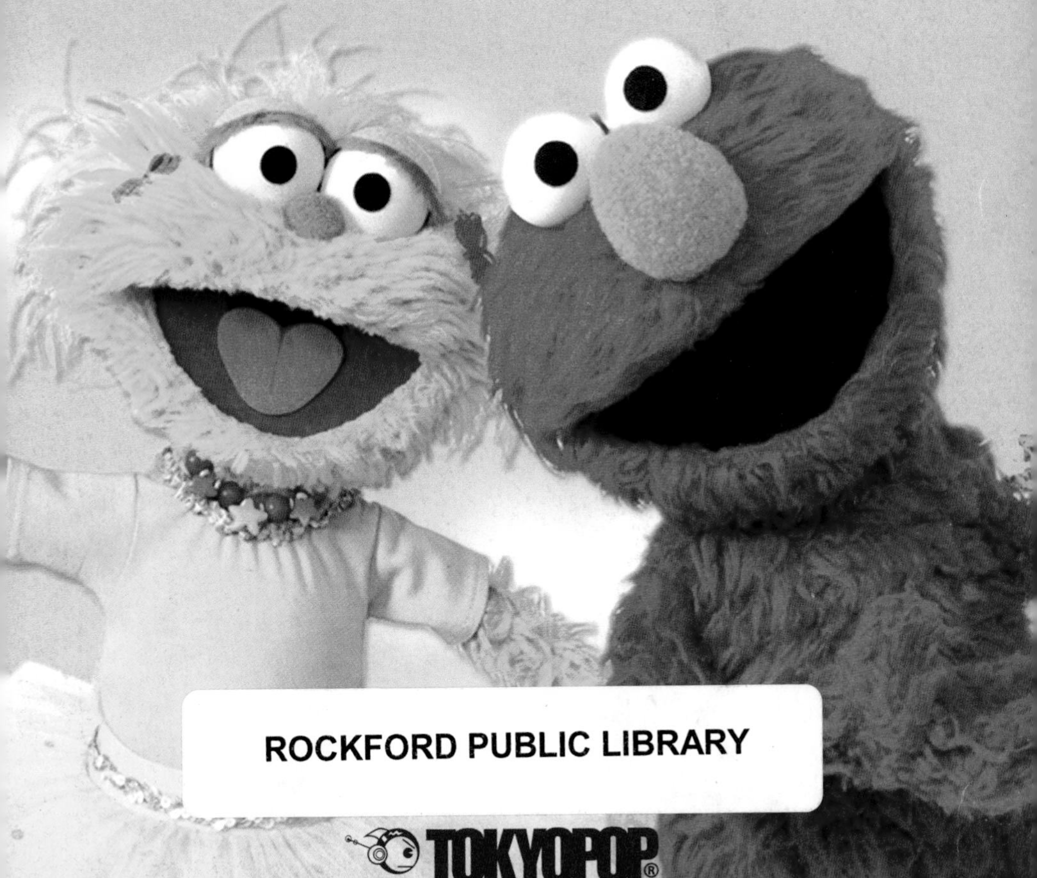

TOKYOPOP

HAMBURG • LONDON • LOS ANGELES • TOKYO

SESAME STREET

MEET YOUR FRIENDS...

ELMO

Elmo is a monster who's the same color as a fire truck or a stop sign. He's very ticklish. Are you?

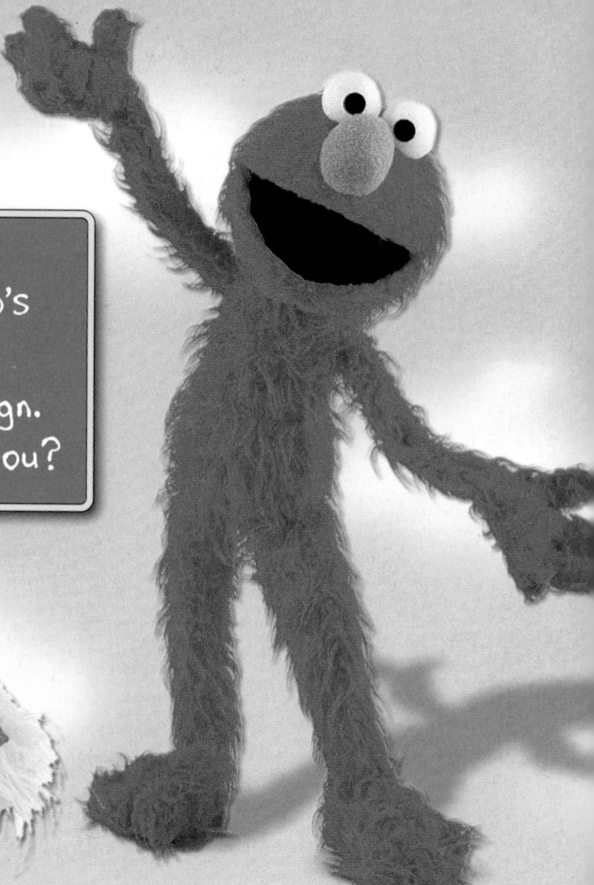

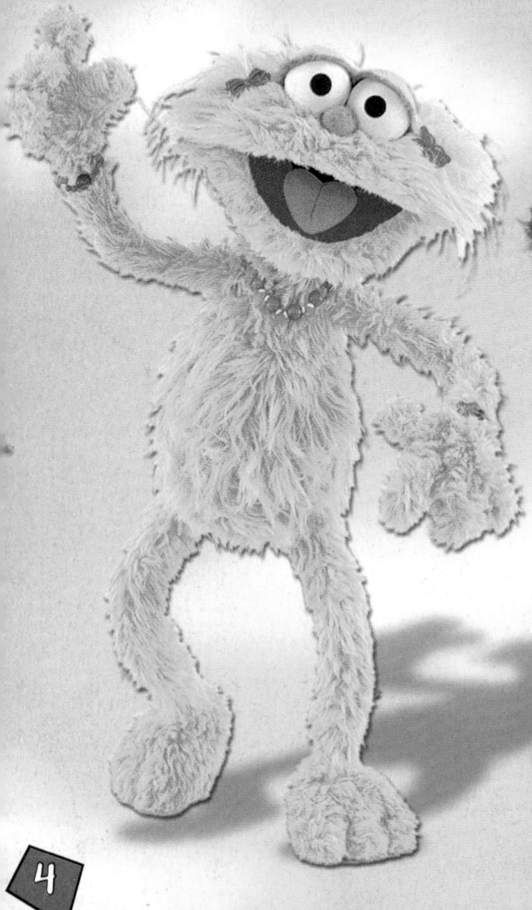

ZOE

She's a funny, furry monster who loves sharing with her best friend, Elmo.

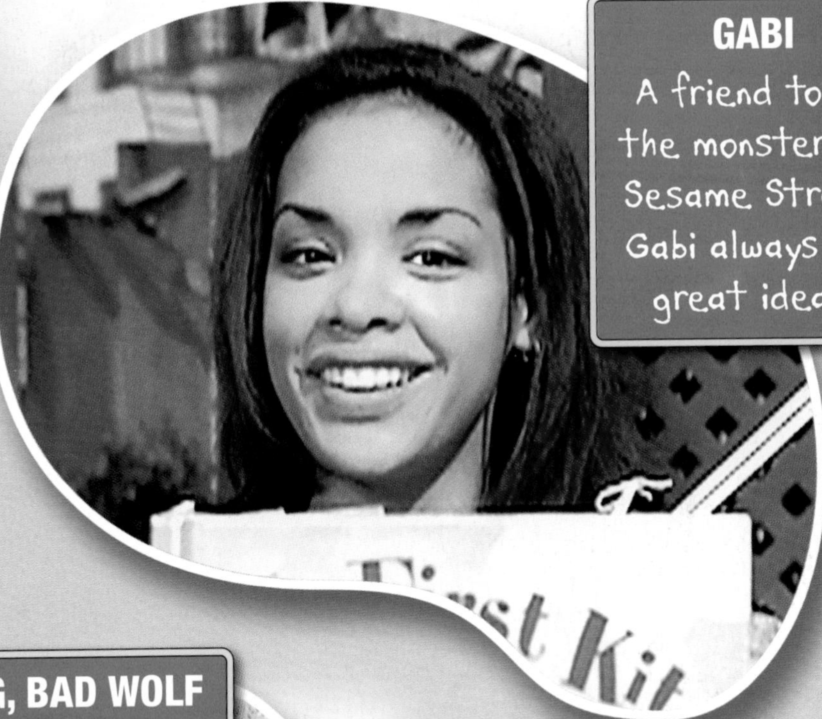

GABI

A friend to all the monsters on Sesame Street, Gabi always has great ideas.

BIG, BAD WOLF

He's not all that big and not all that bad.

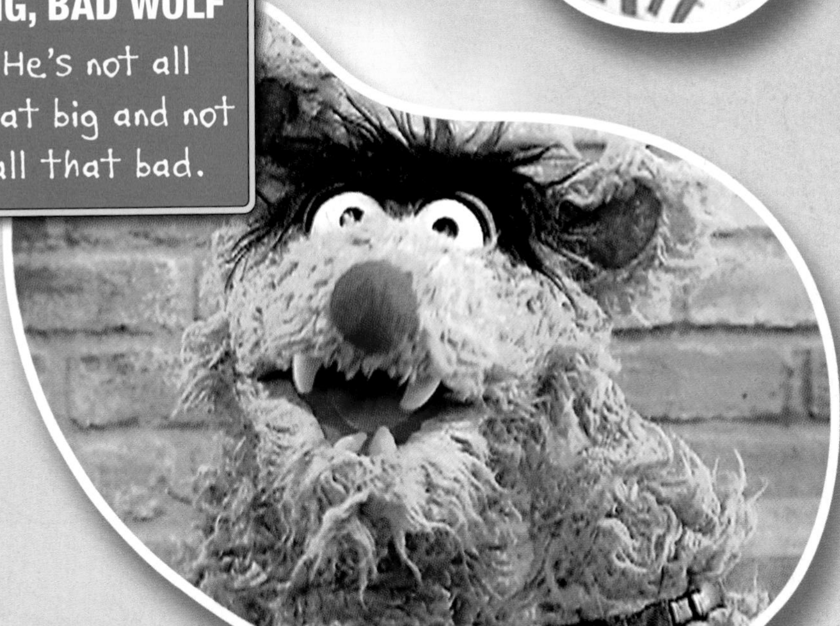

IT ALL BEGAN WHEN ELMO AND ZOE SAW A SHOW ABOUT KITES.

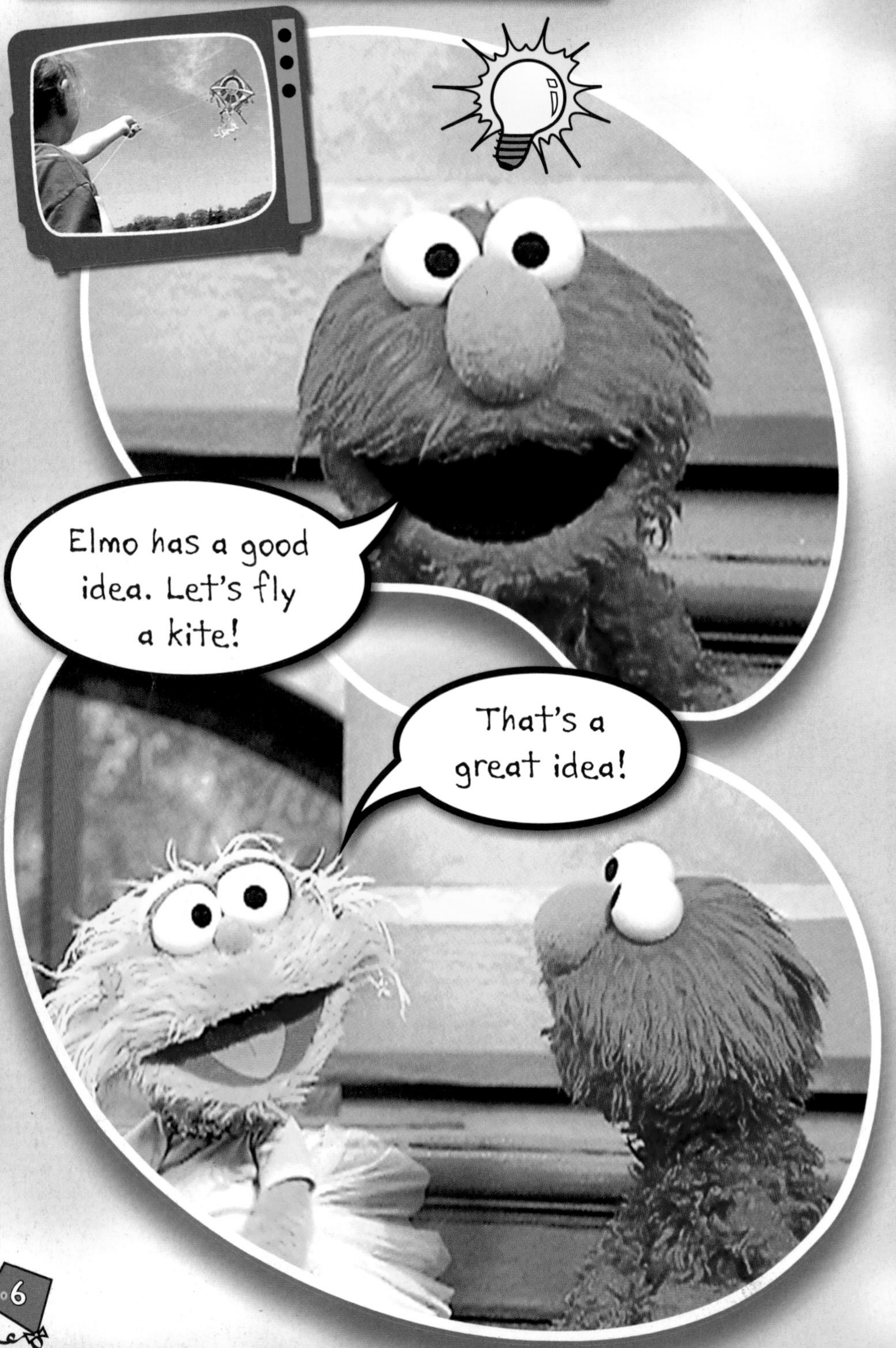
Elmo has a good idea. Let's fly a kite!
That's a great idea!

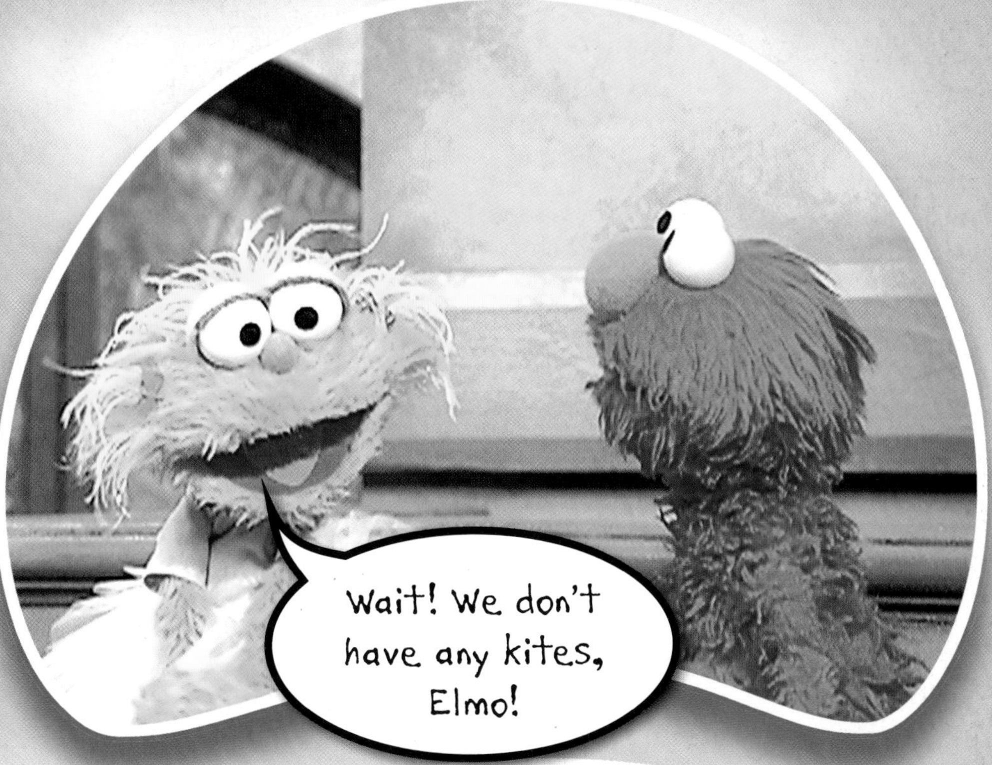
Wait! We don't have any kites, Elmo!

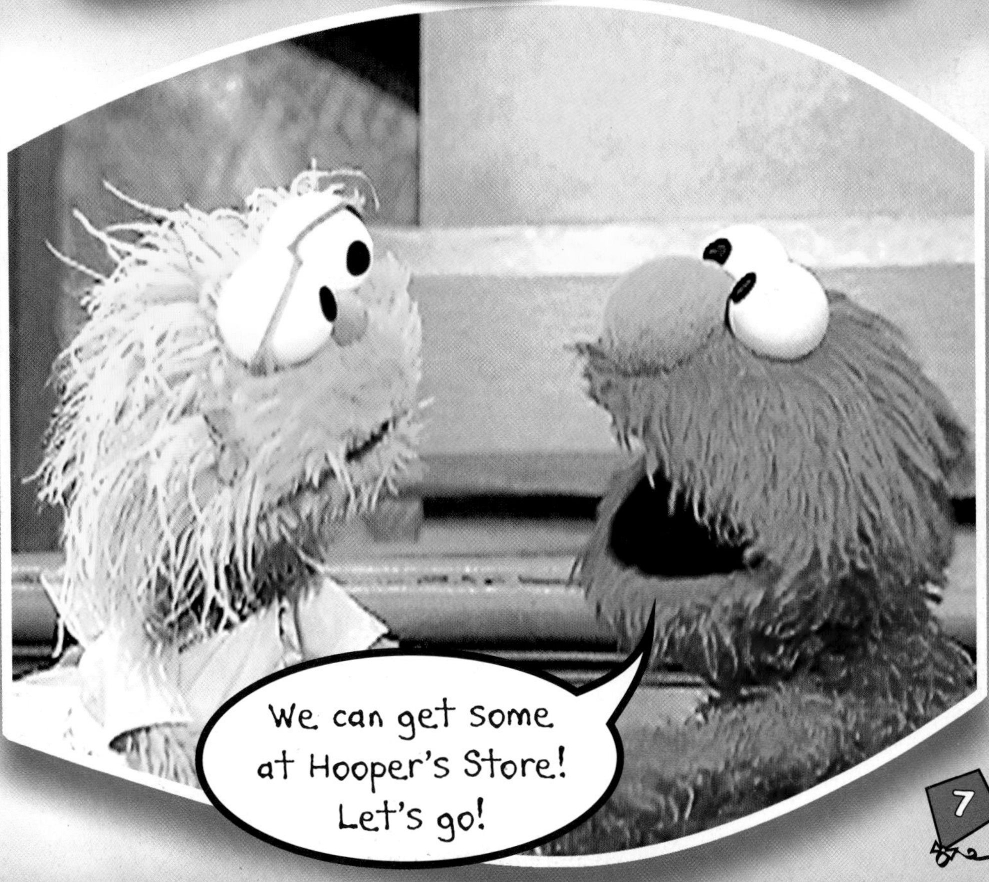
We can get some at Hooper's Store! Let's go!

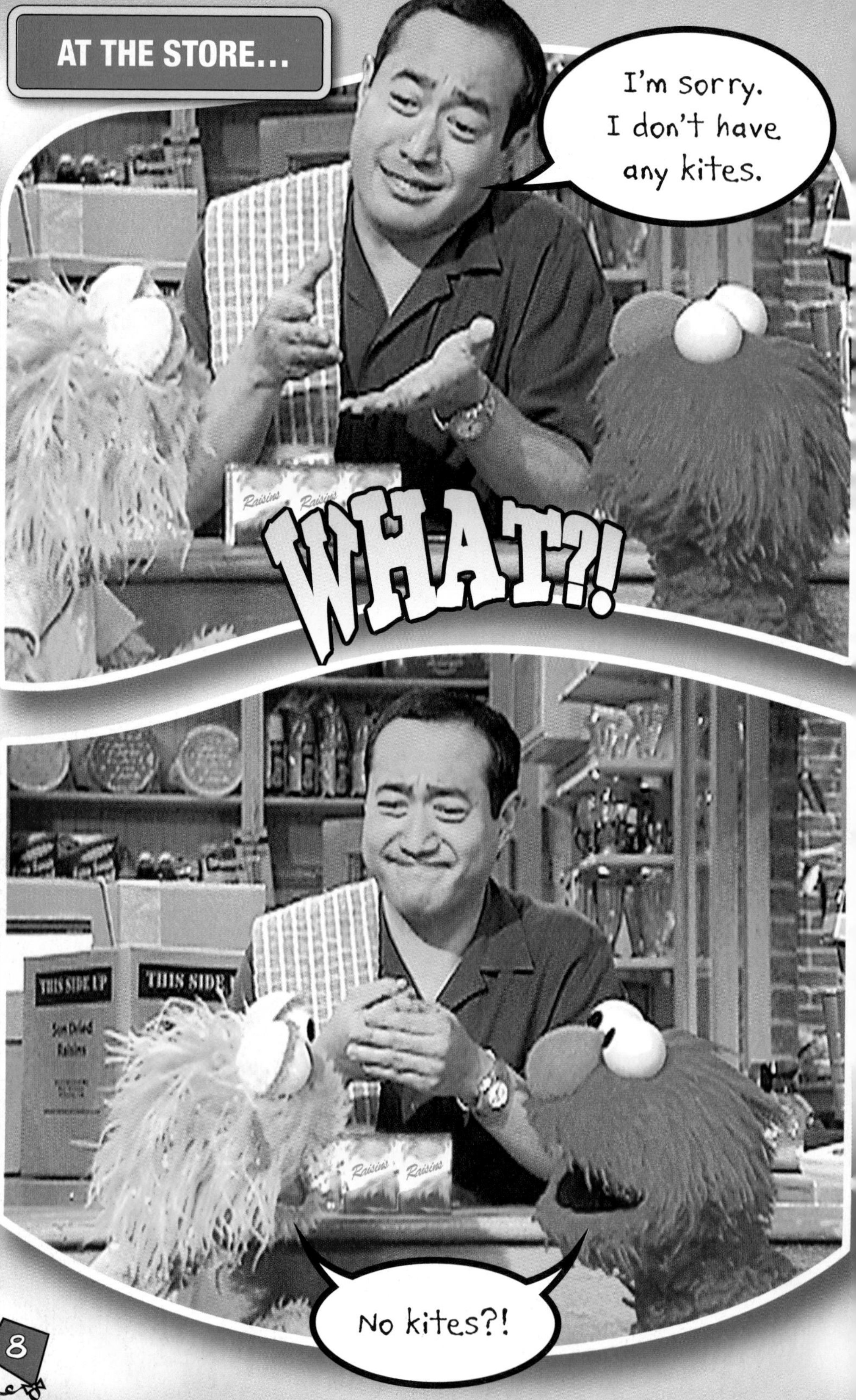
AT THE STORE...
I'm sorry. I don't have any kites.
WHAT?!
No kites?!

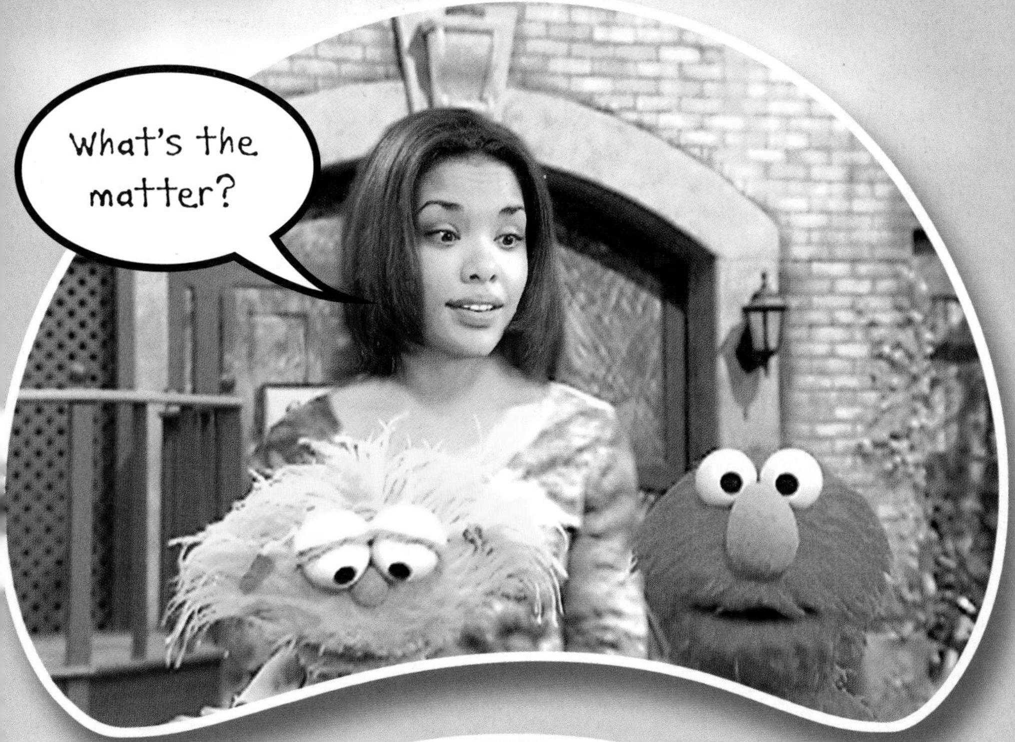
What's the matter?

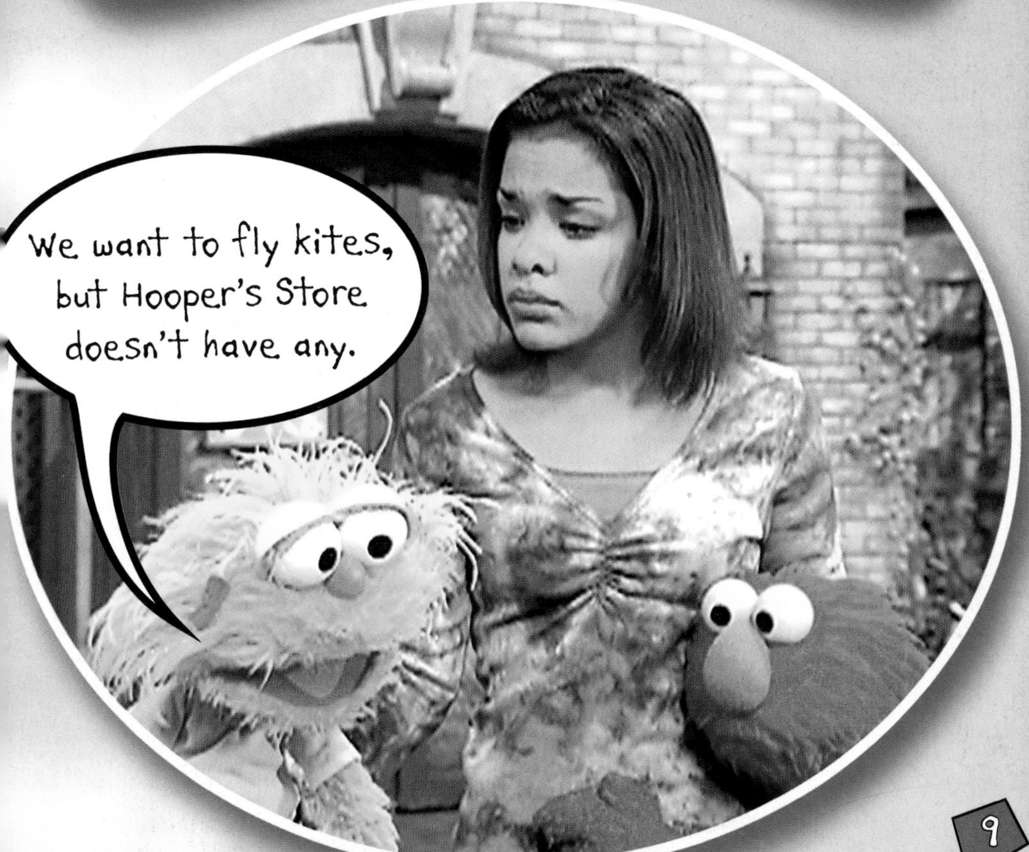
We want to fly kites, but Hooper's Store doesn't have any.

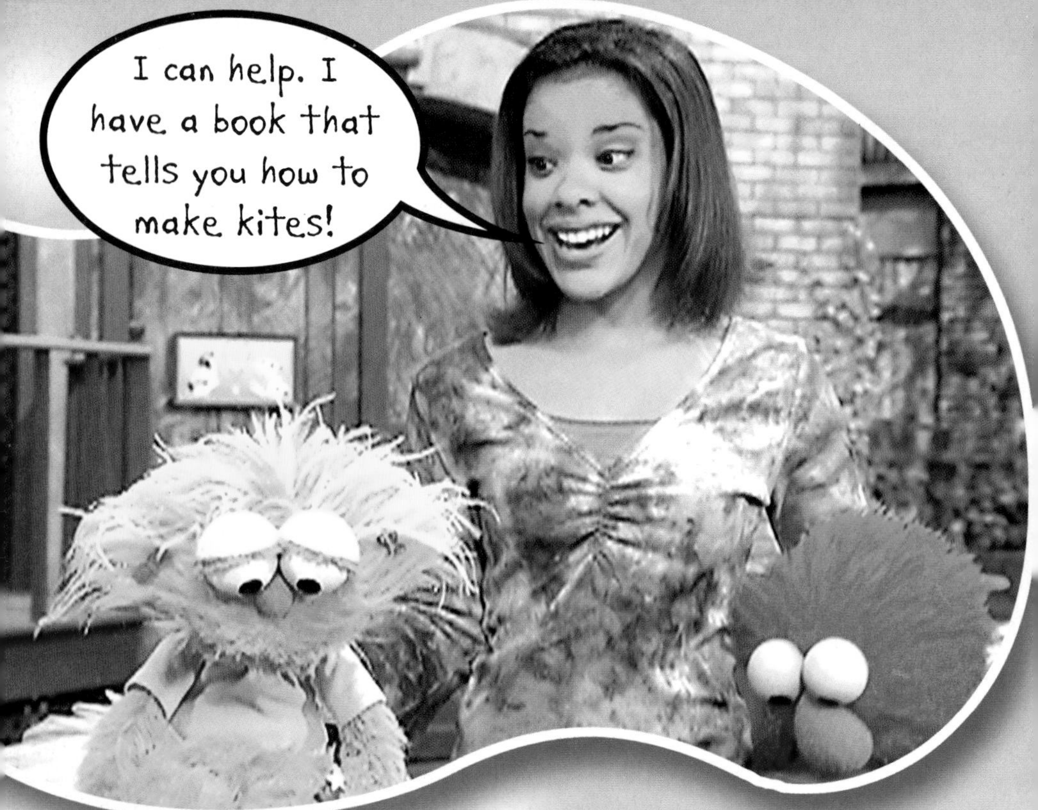
I can help. I have a book that tells you how to make kites!

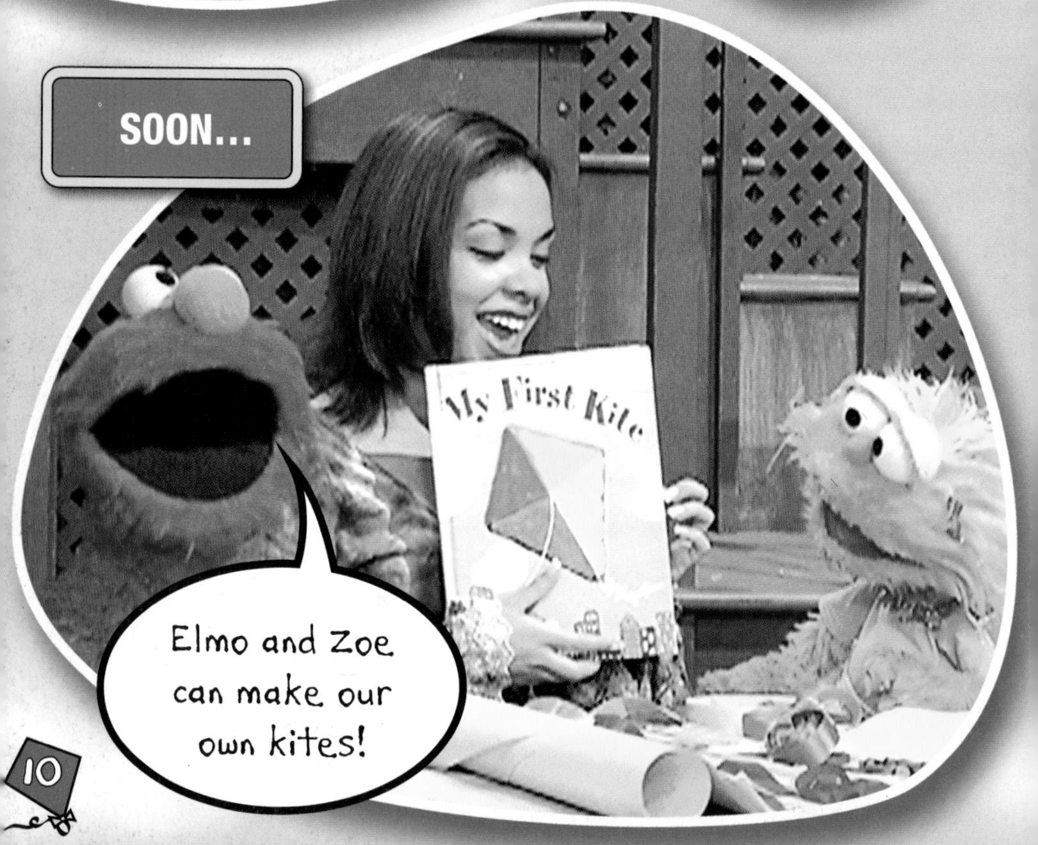
SOON...
My First Kite
Elmo and Zoe can make our own kites!

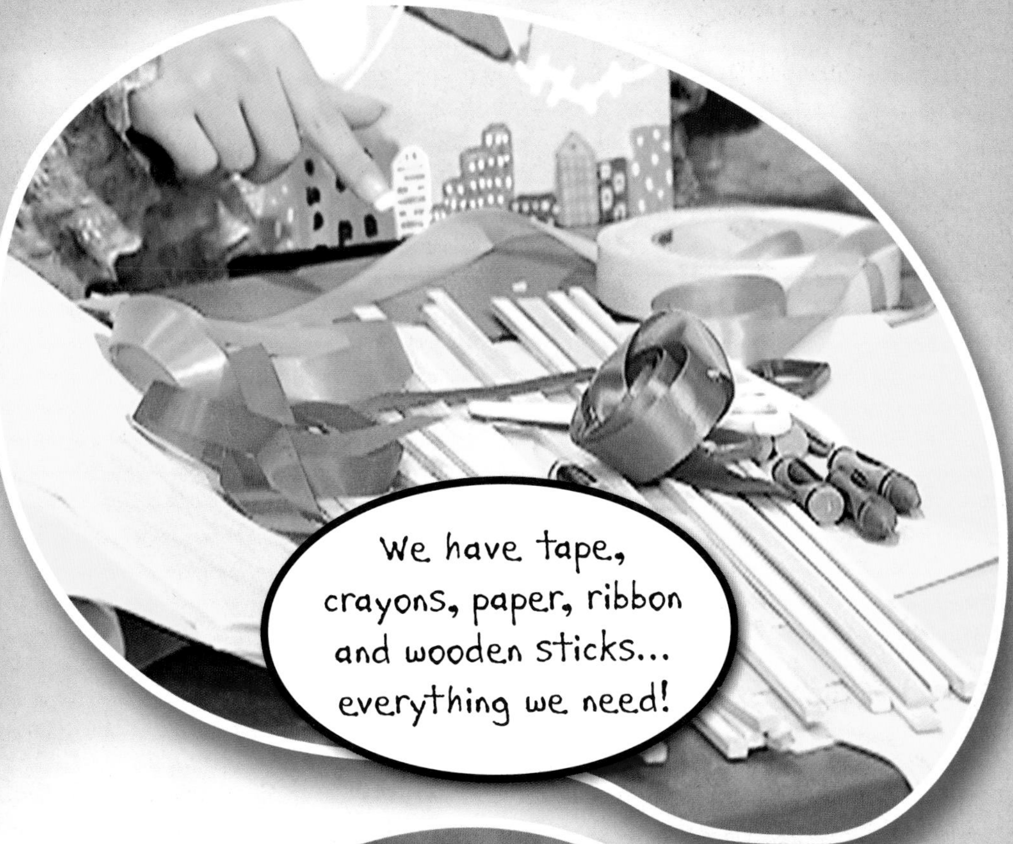
We have tape, crayons, paper, ribbon and wooden sticks... everything we need!

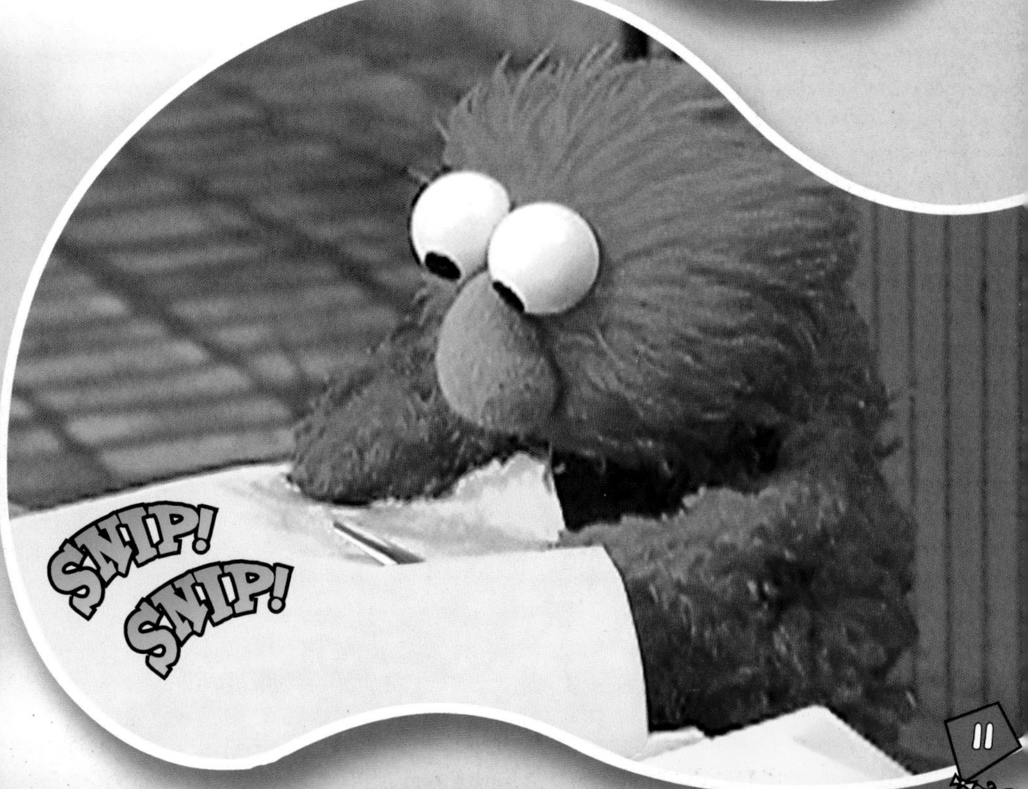
SNIP! SNIP!

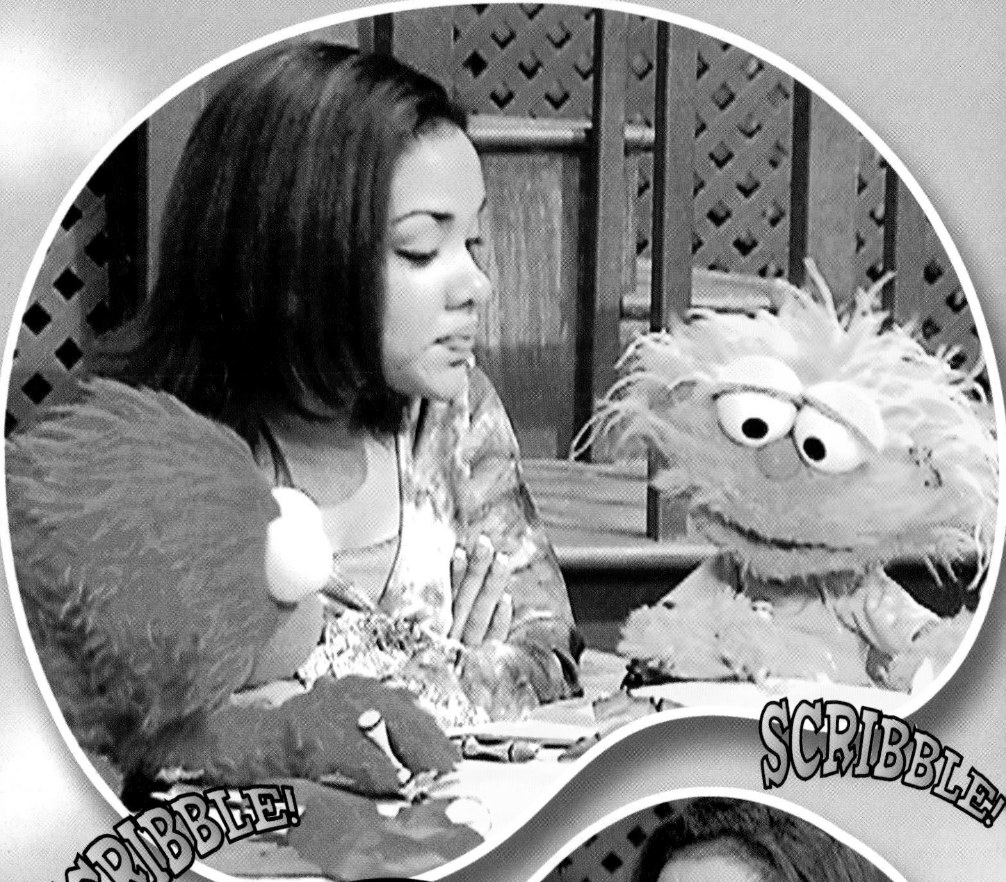
SCRIBBLE!
SCRIBBLE!

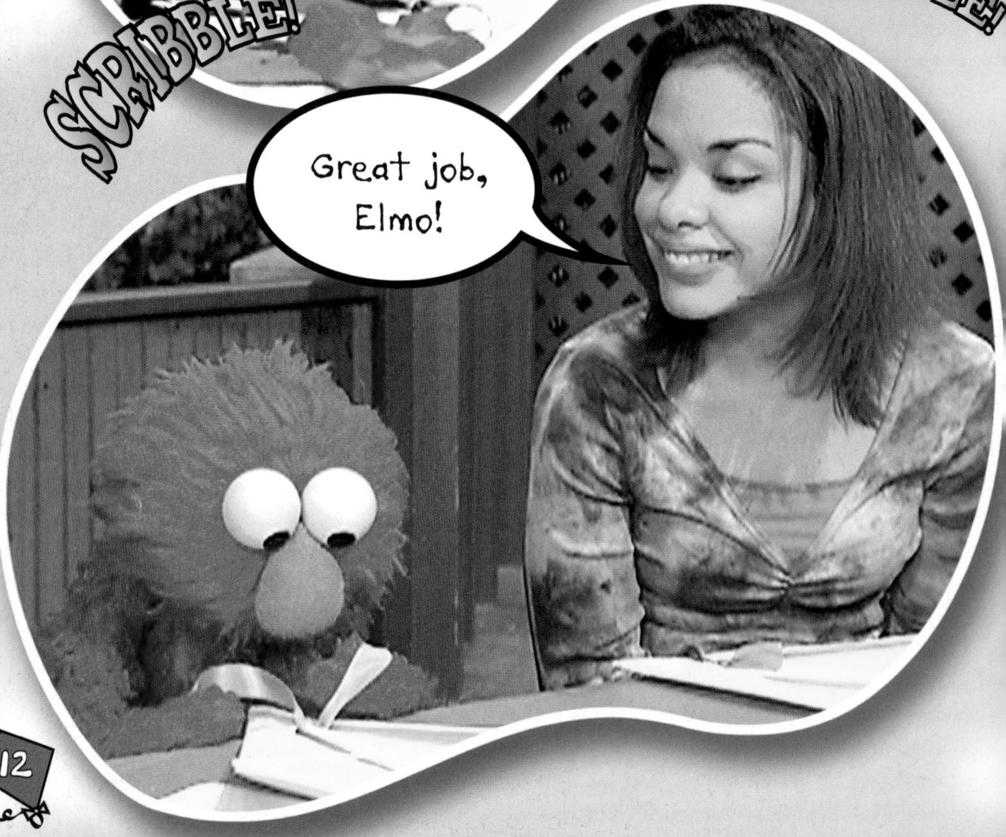
Great job, Elmo!

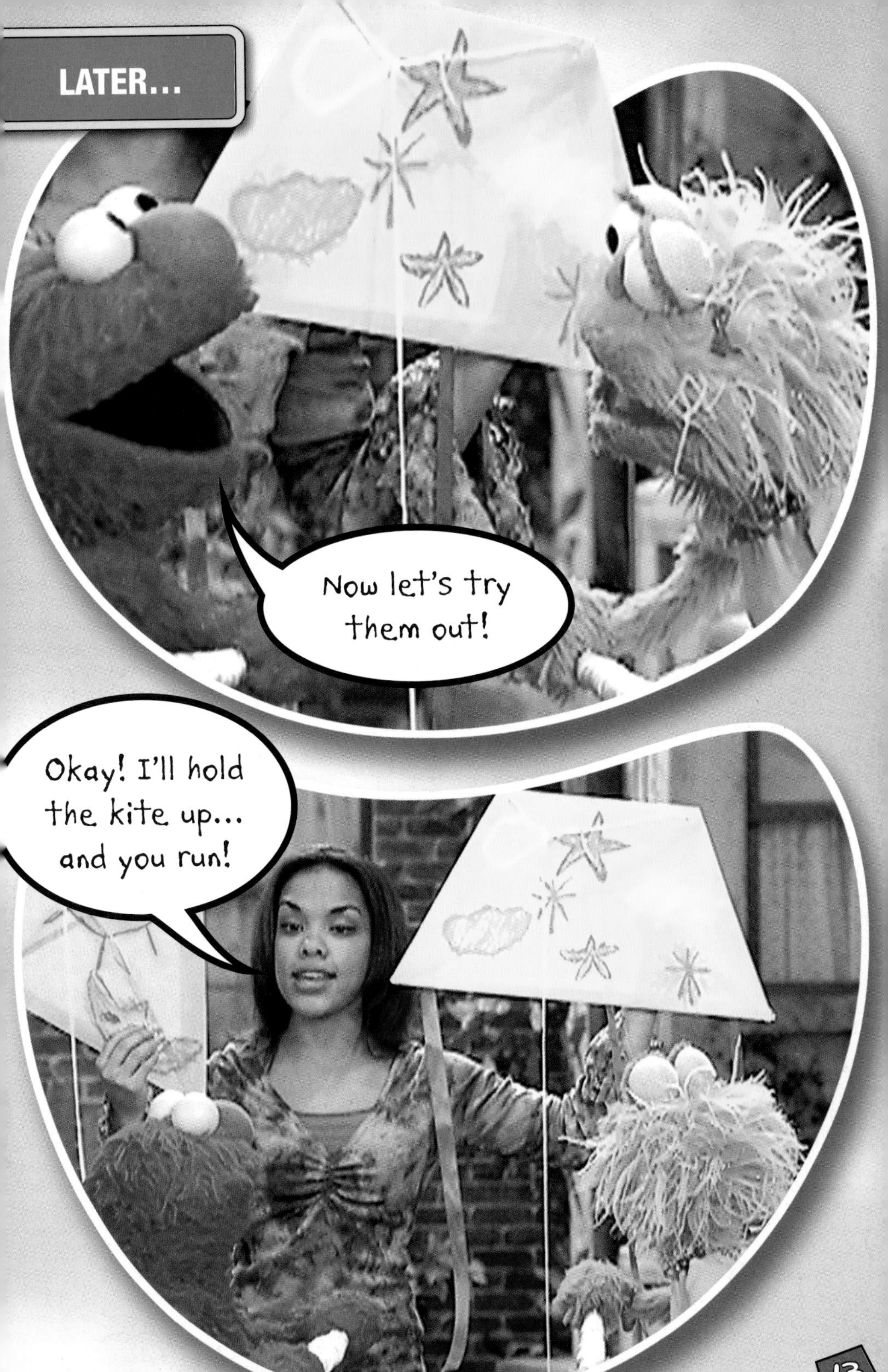
LATER...
Now let's try them out!
Okay! I'll hold the kite up... and you run!

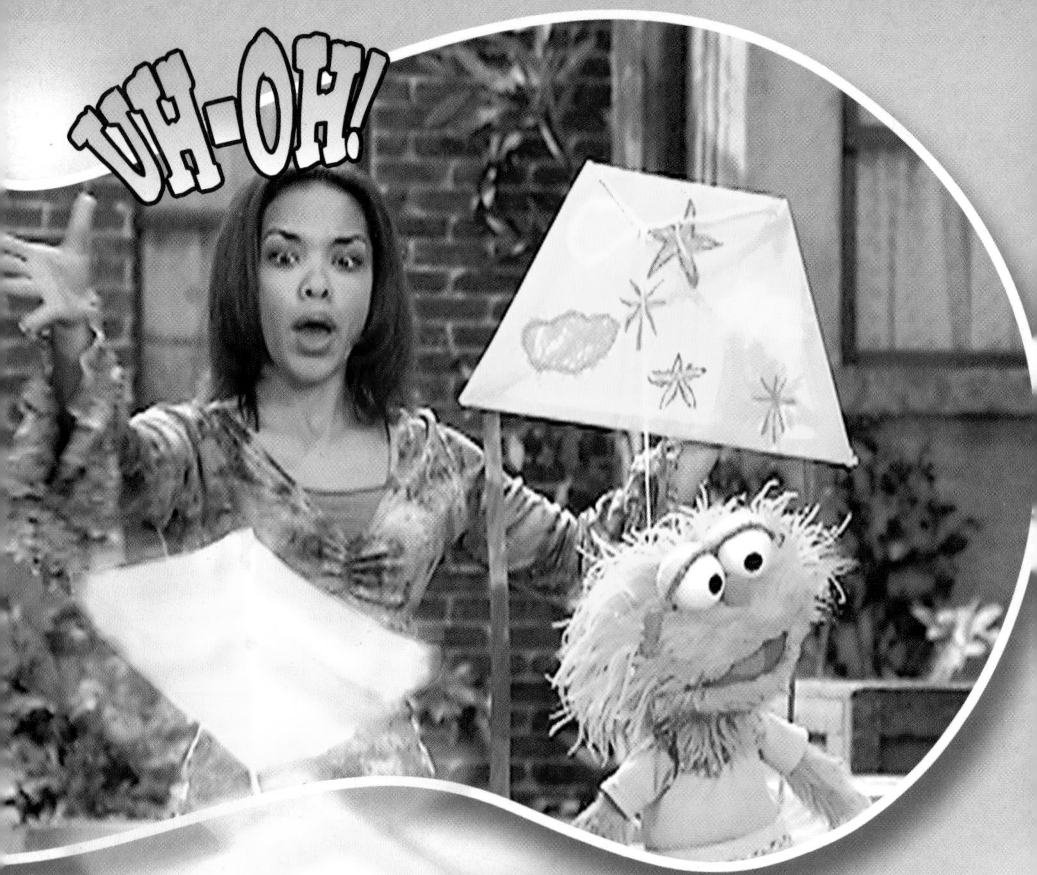
UH-OH!

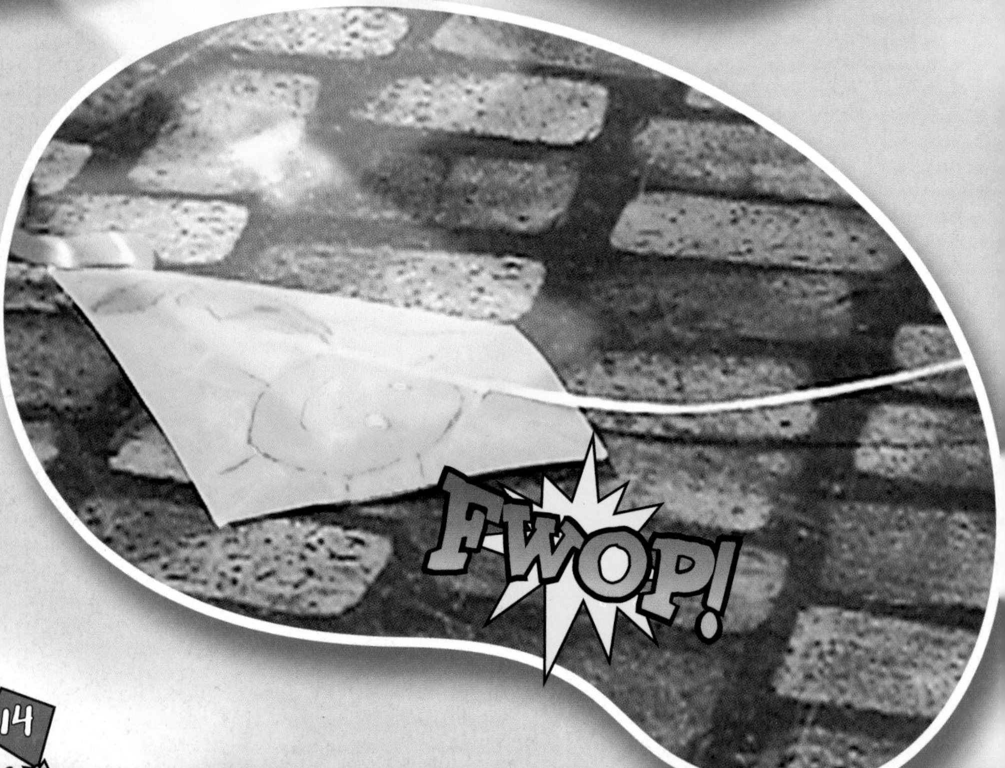
FWOP!

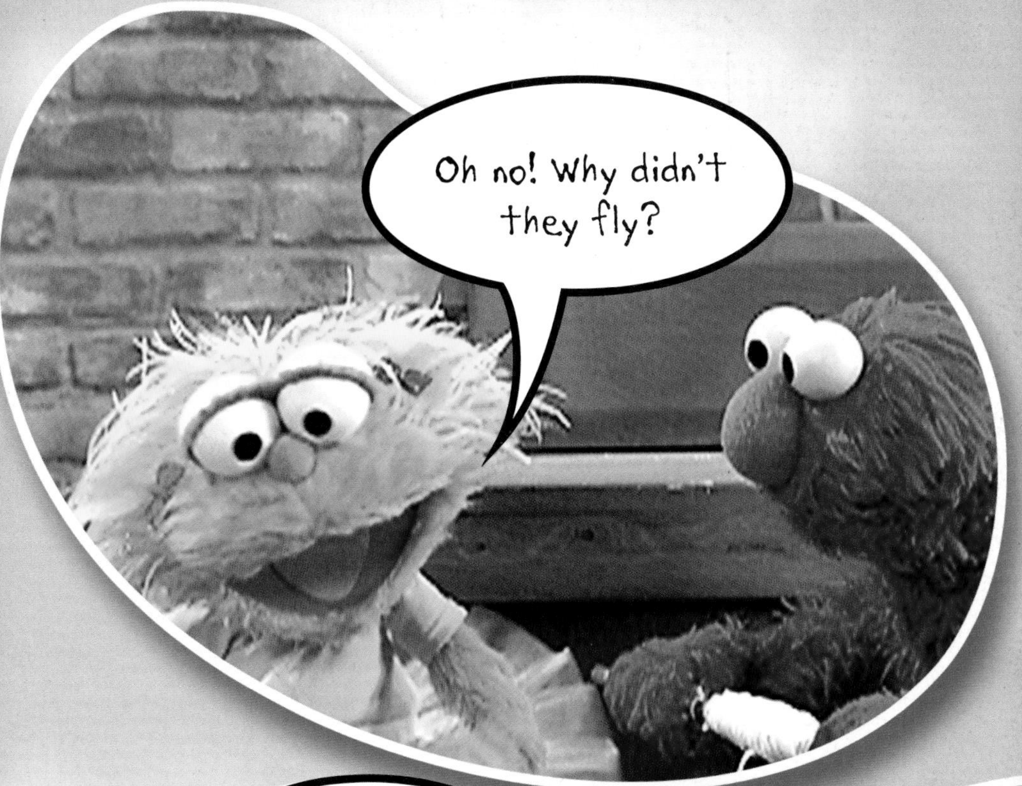
Oh no! Why didn't they fly?

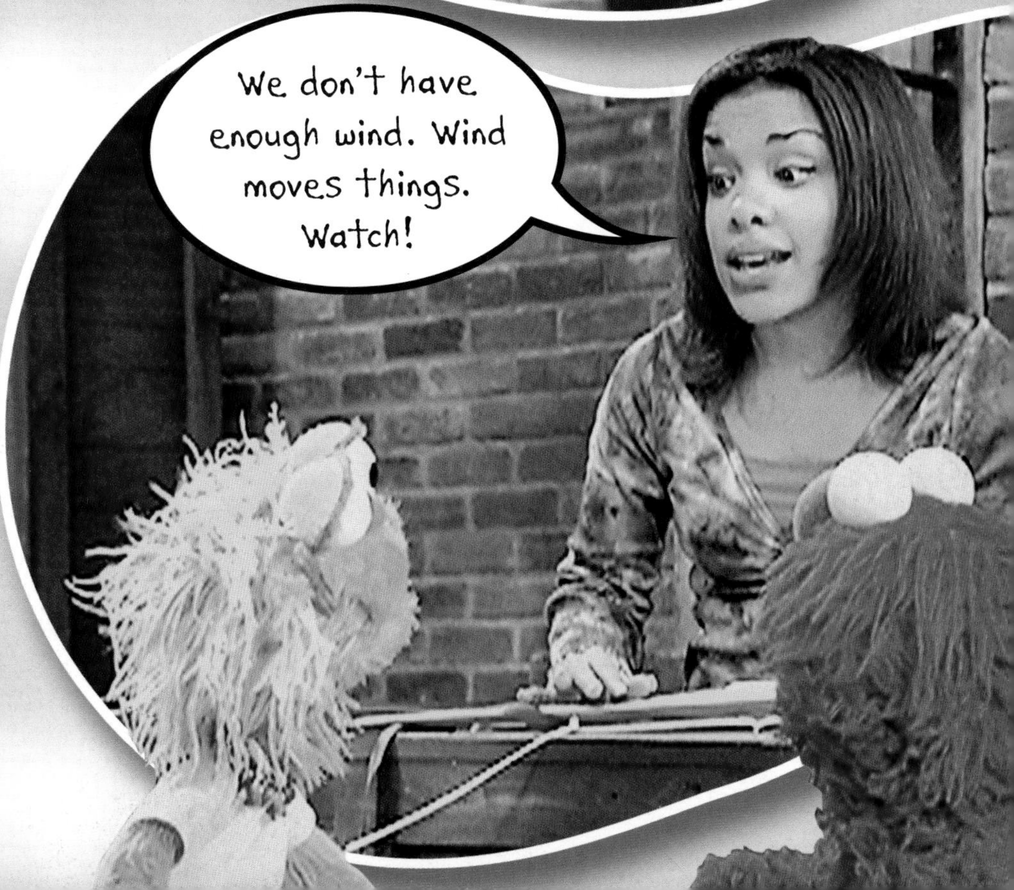
We don't have enough wind. Wind moves things. Watch!

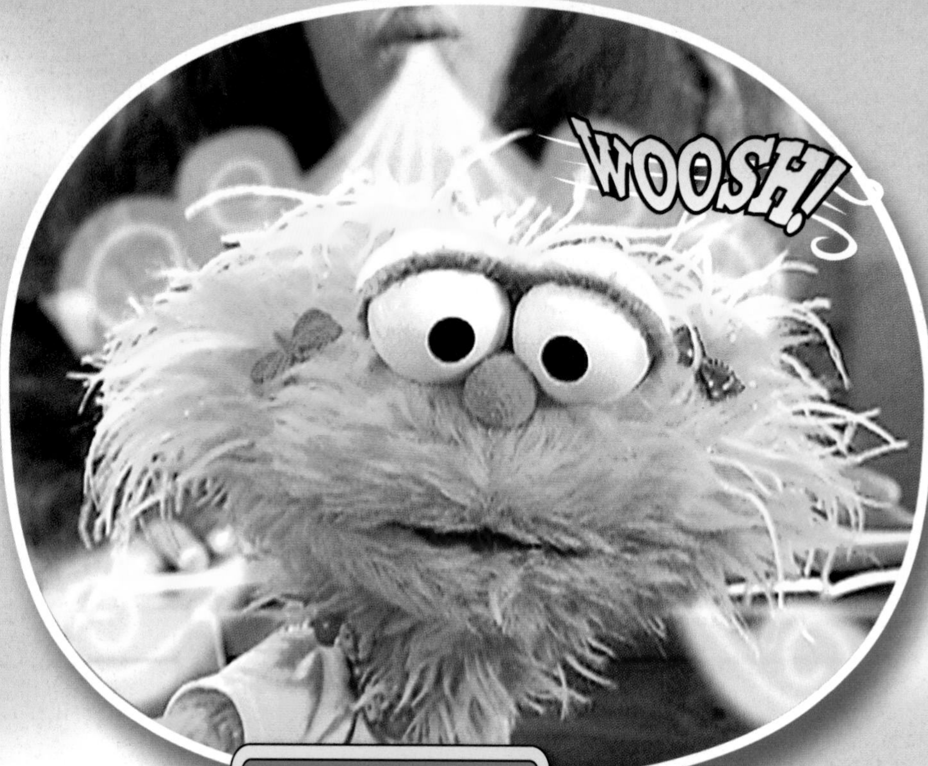
WOOSH!
AND ZOE'S HAIR *MOVED!*

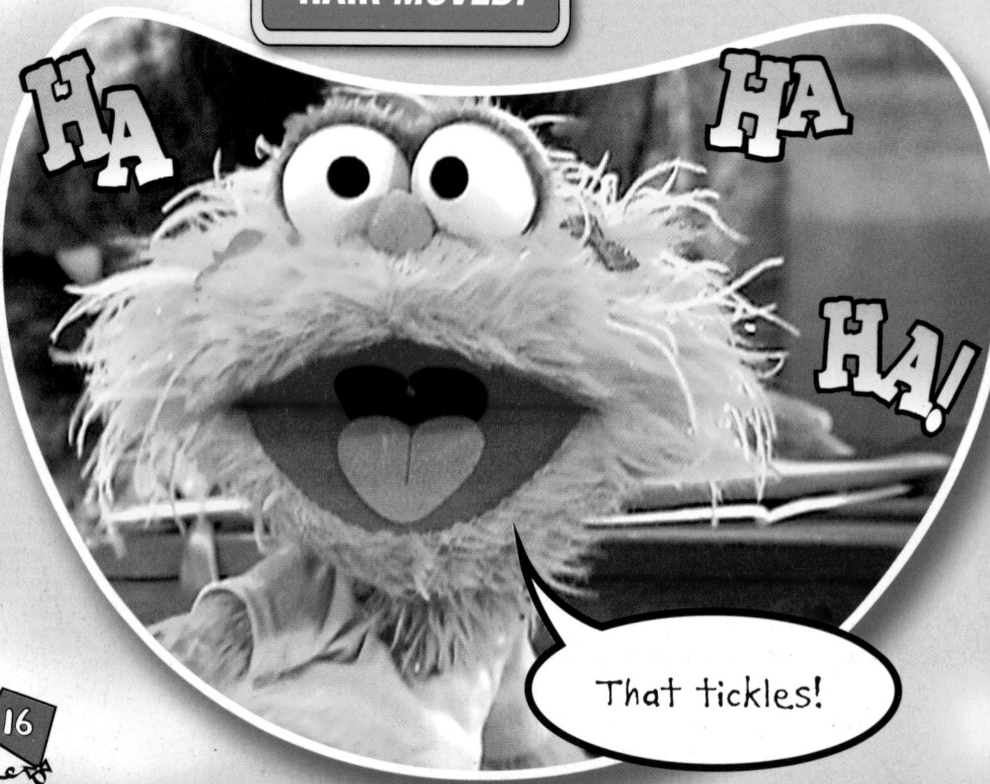
HA
HA
HA!
That tickles!

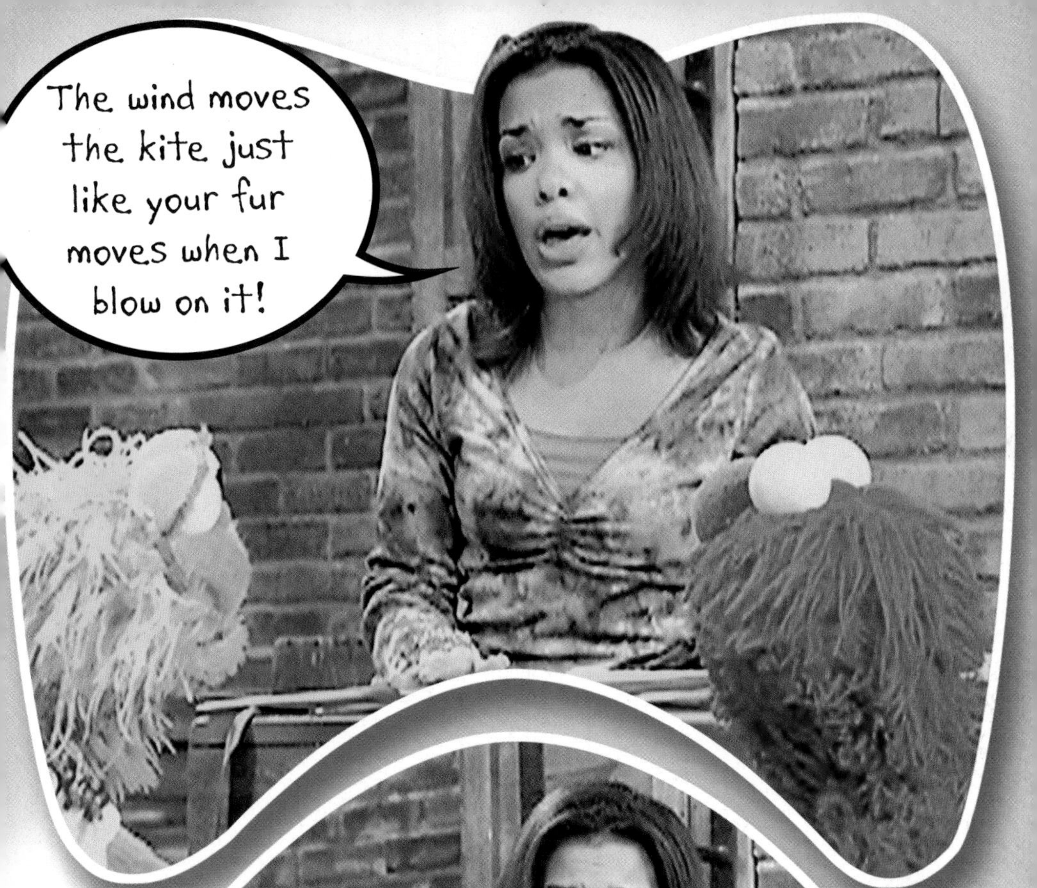
The wind moves the kite just like your fur moves when I blow on it!

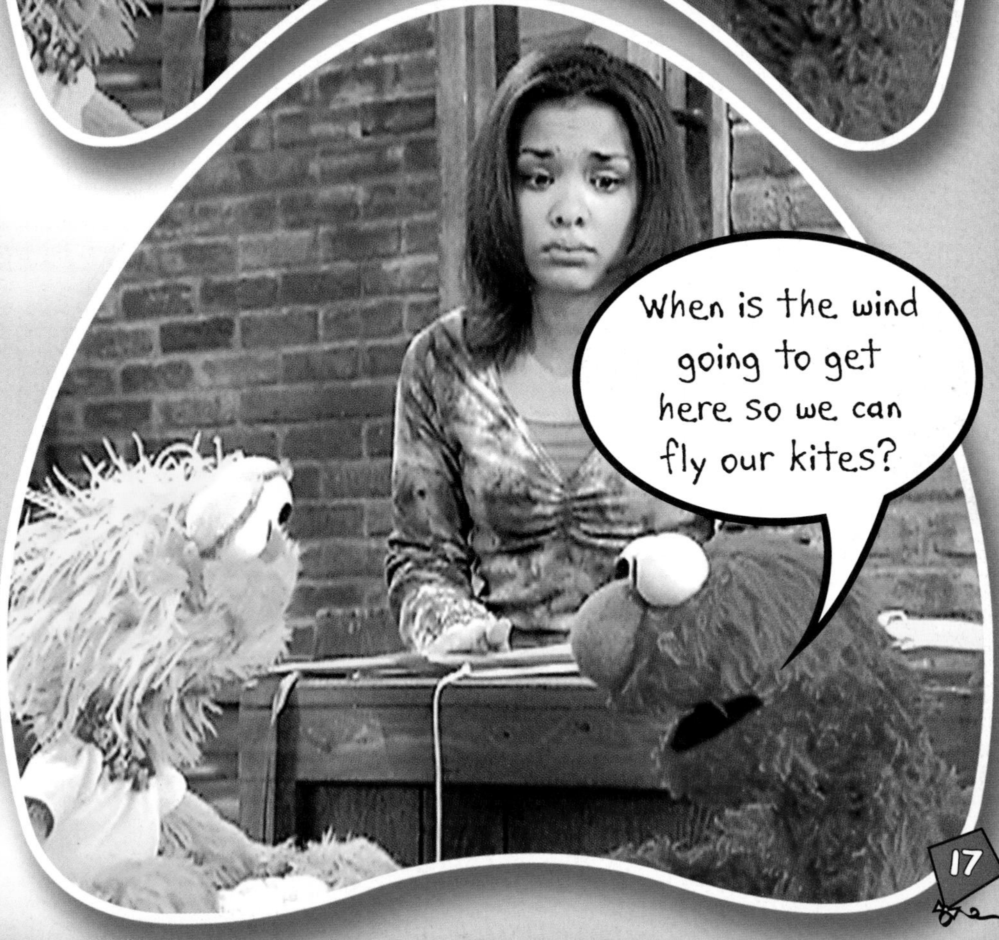
When is the wind going to get here so we can fly our kites?

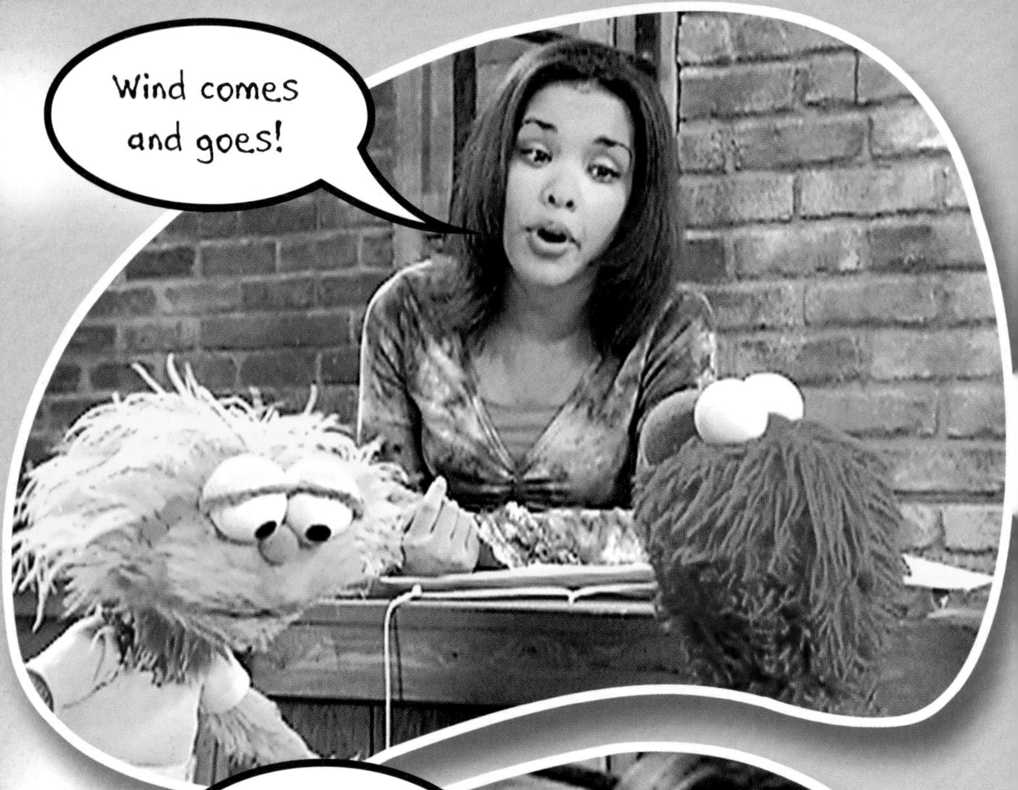
Wind comes and goes!

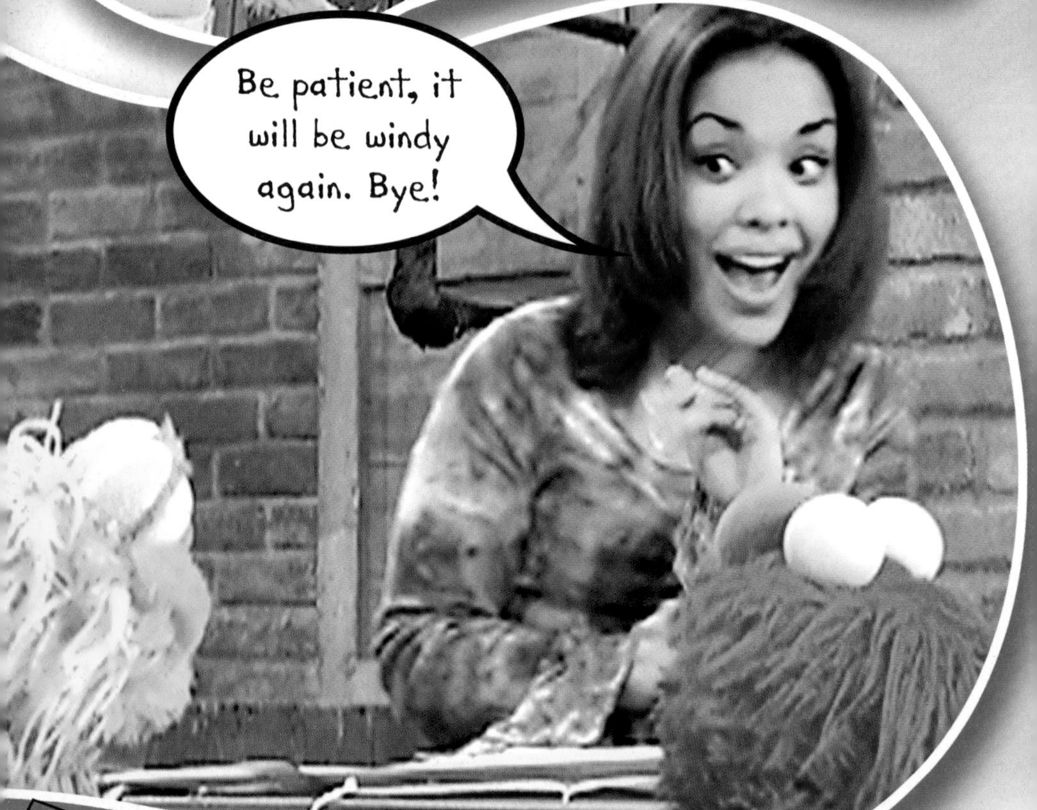
Be patient, it will be windy again. Bye!

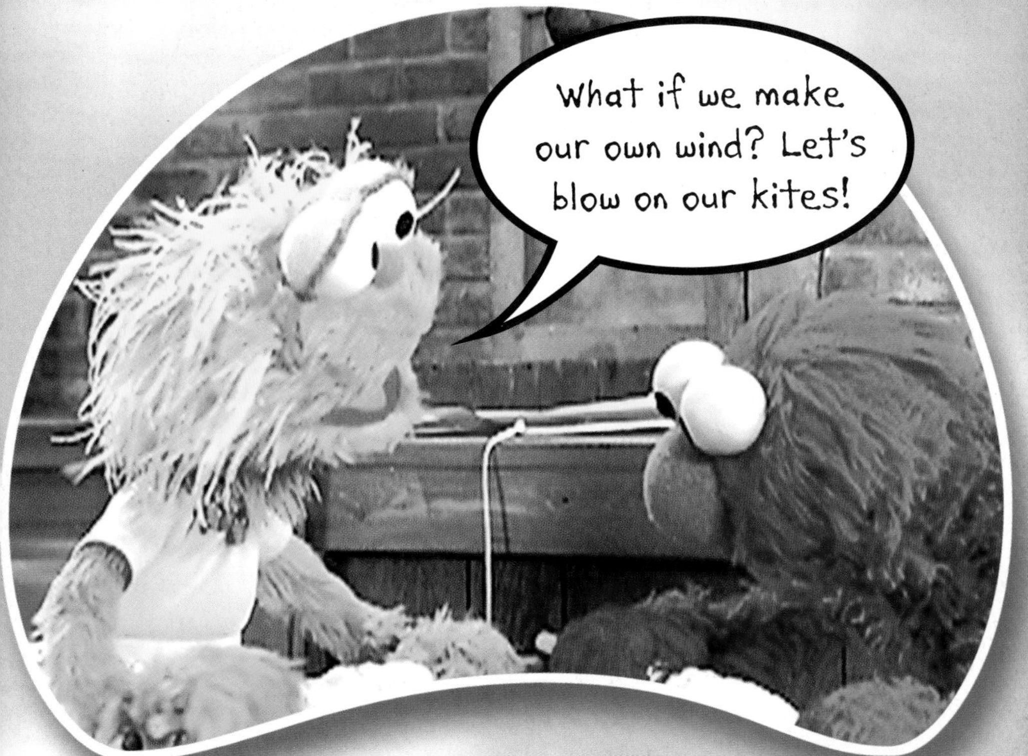
What if we make our own wind? Let's blow on our kites!

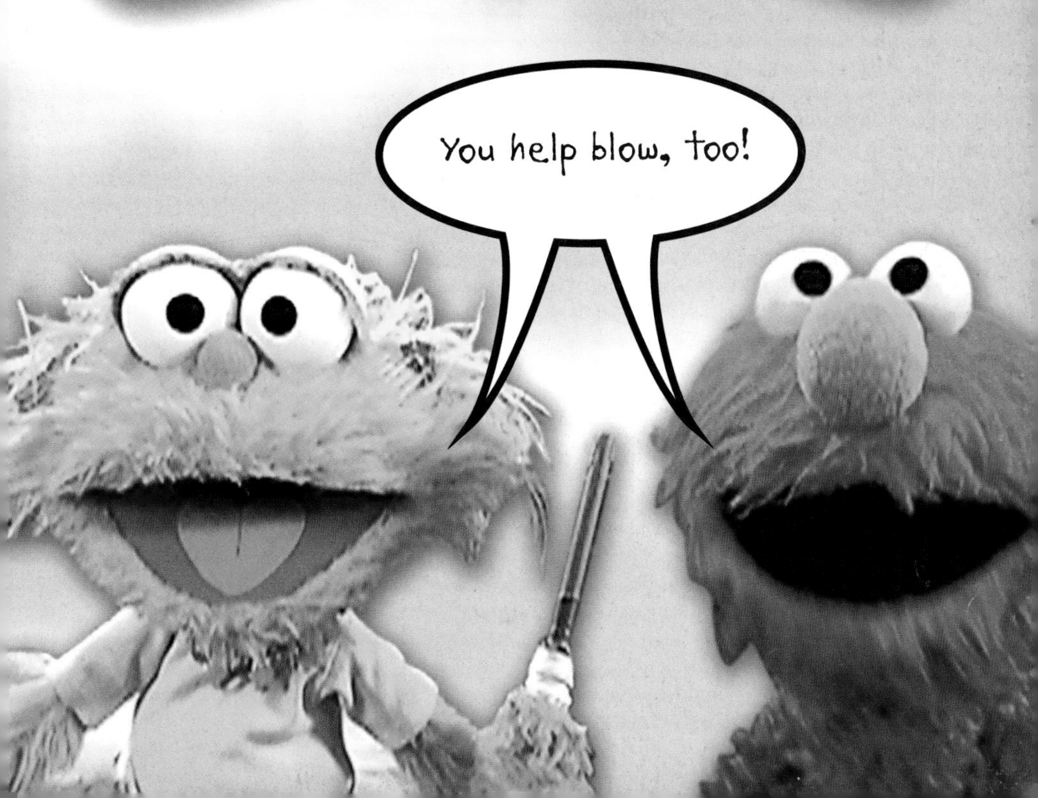
You help blow, too!

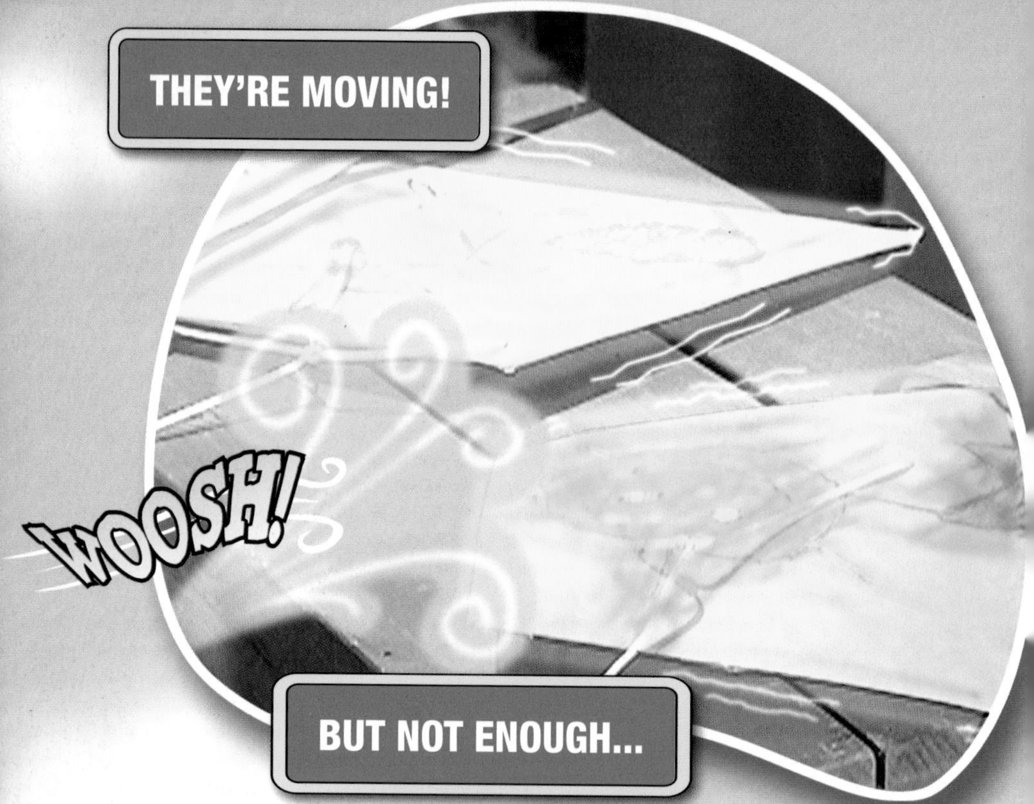
THEY'RE MOVING!
WOOSH!
BUT NOT ENOUGH...

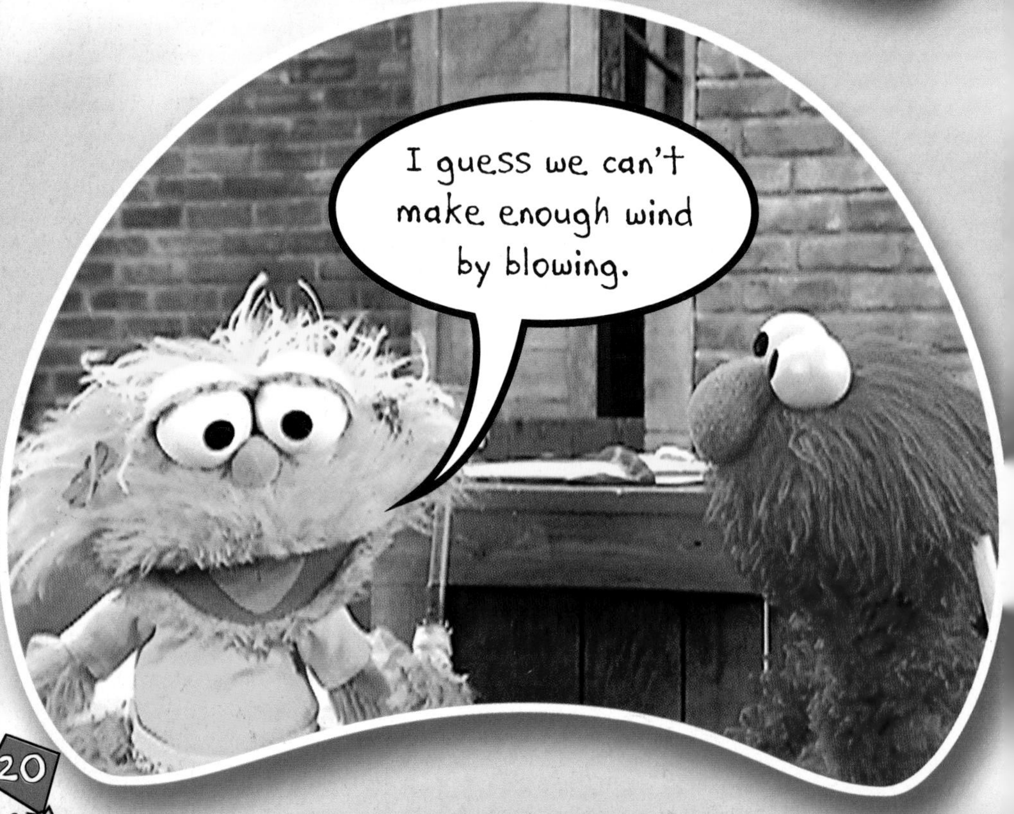
I guess we can't make enough wind by blowing.

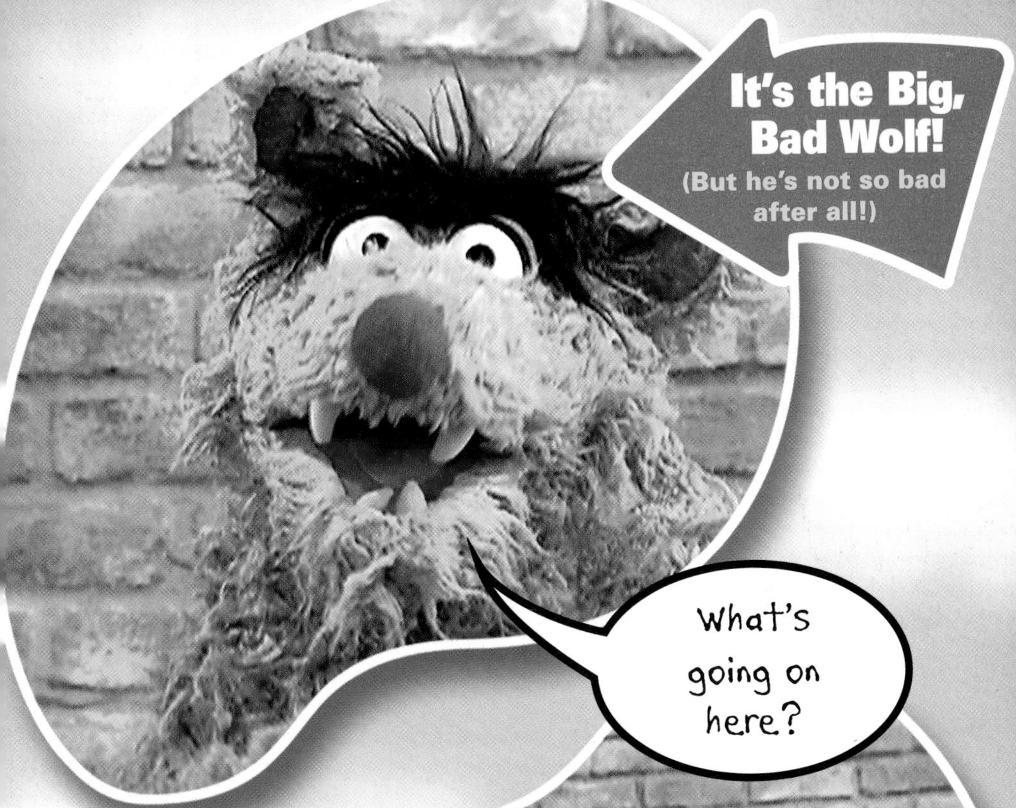

It's the Big, Bad Wolf!
(But he's not so bad after all!)
What's going on here?

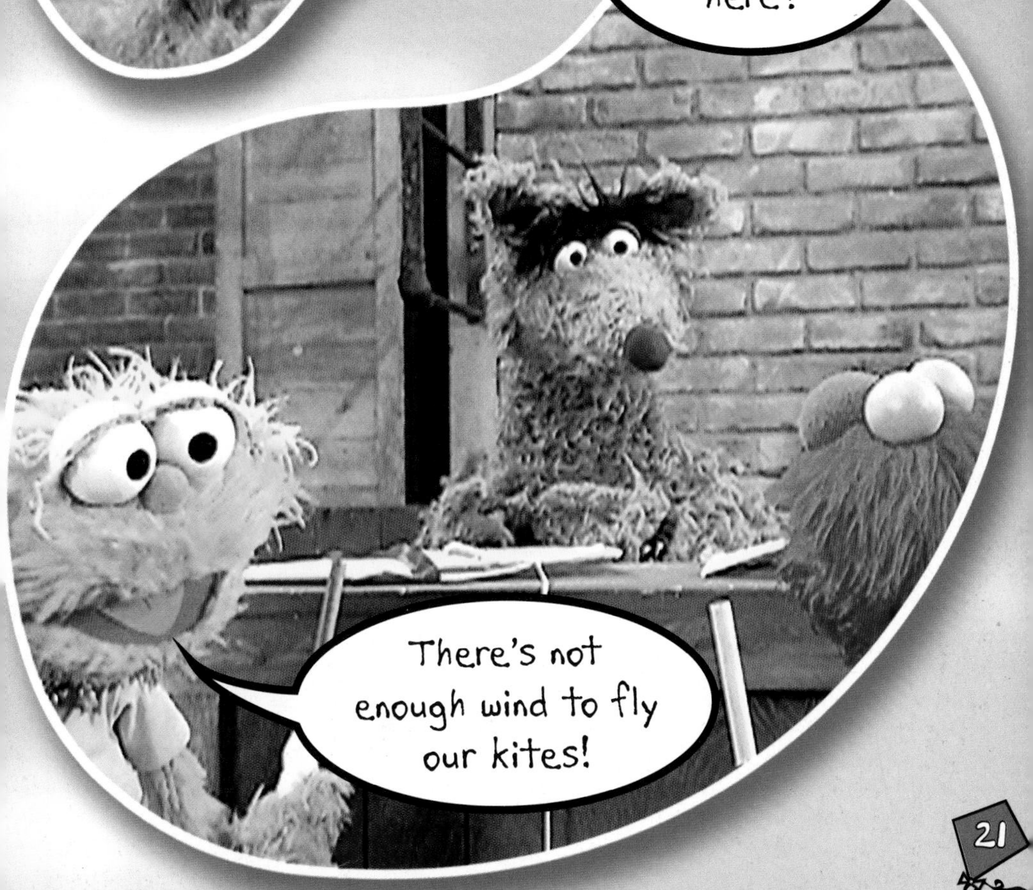

There's not enough wind to fly our kites!

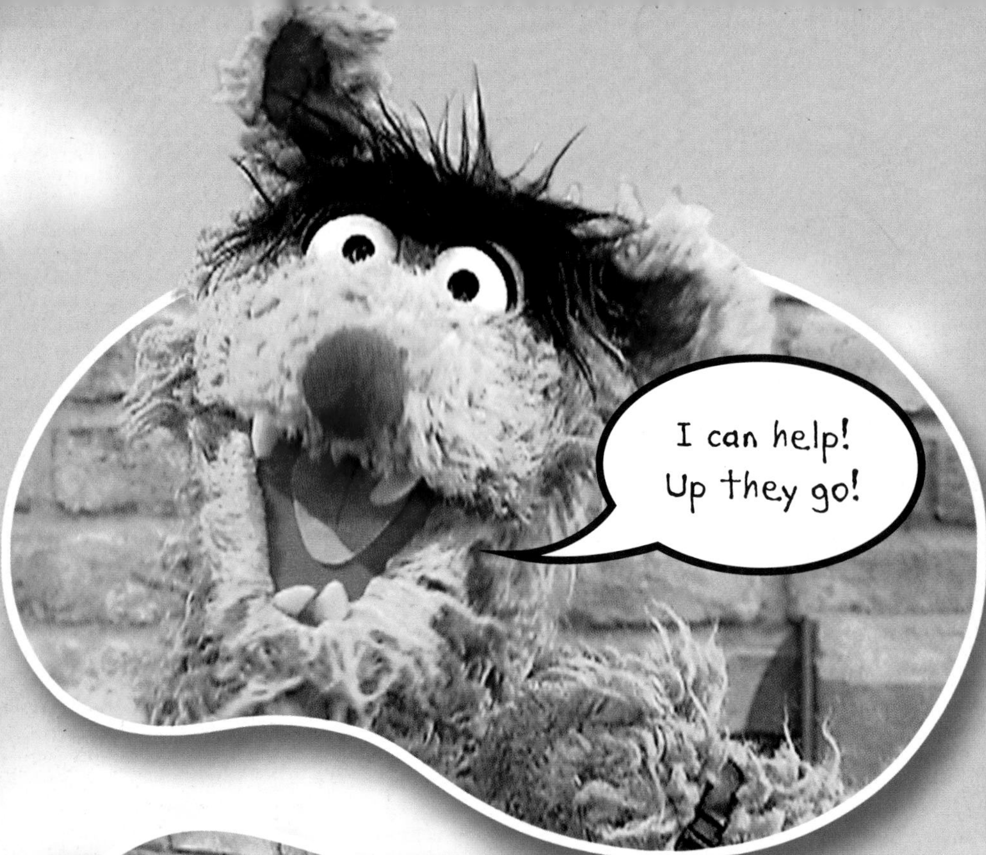
I can help! Up they go!

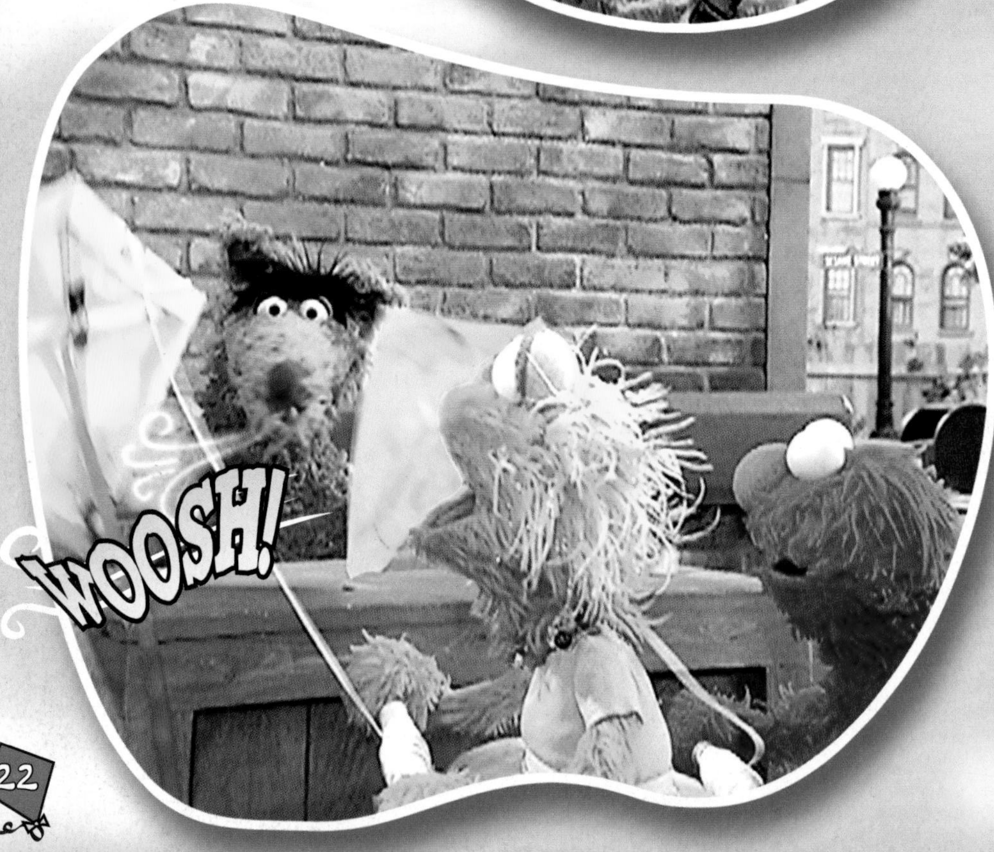
WOOSH!

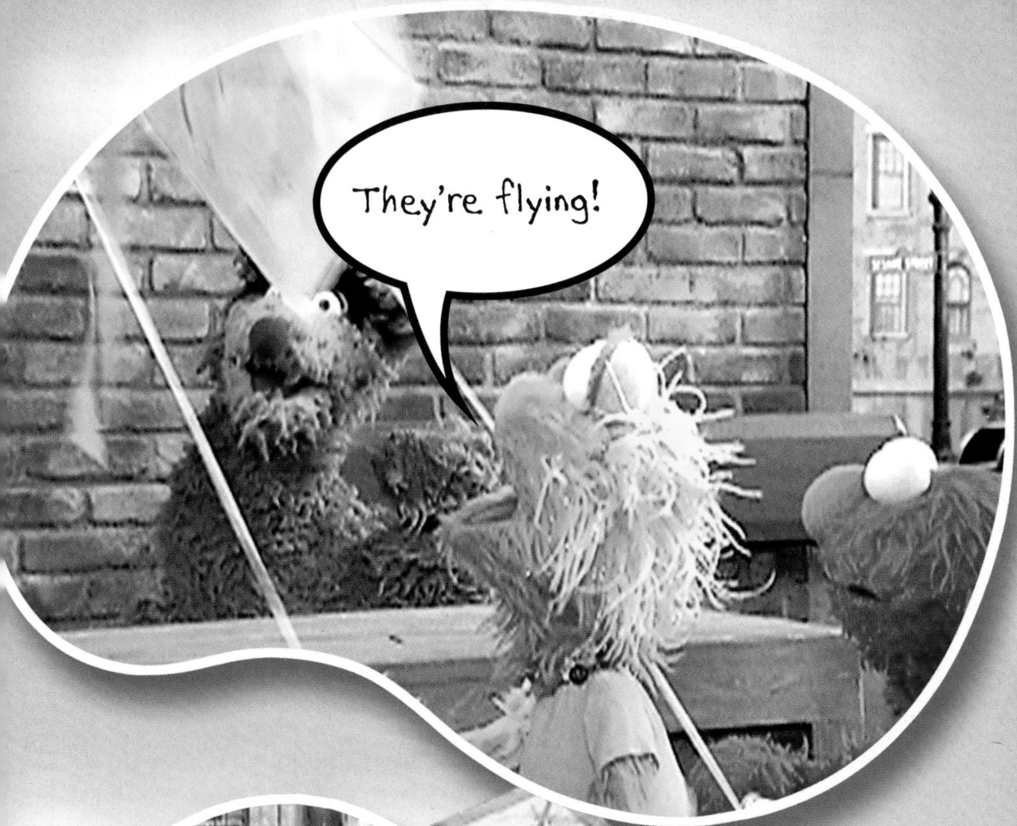
They're flying!

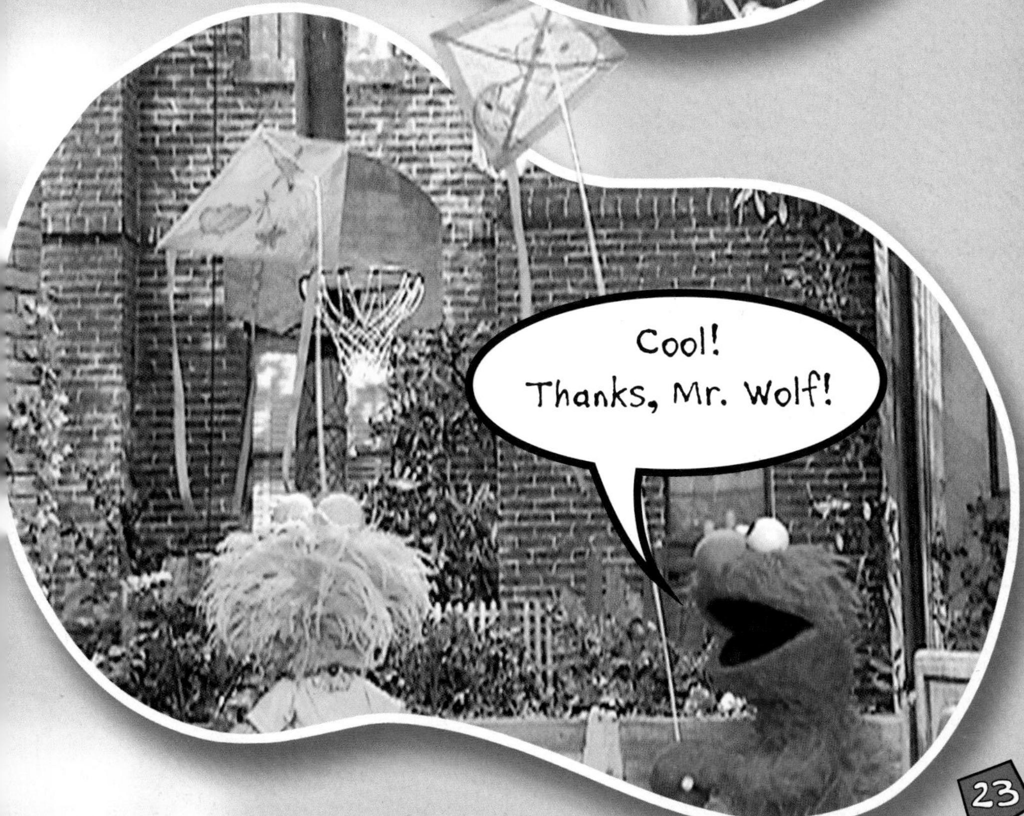
Cool!
Thanks, Mr. Wolf!

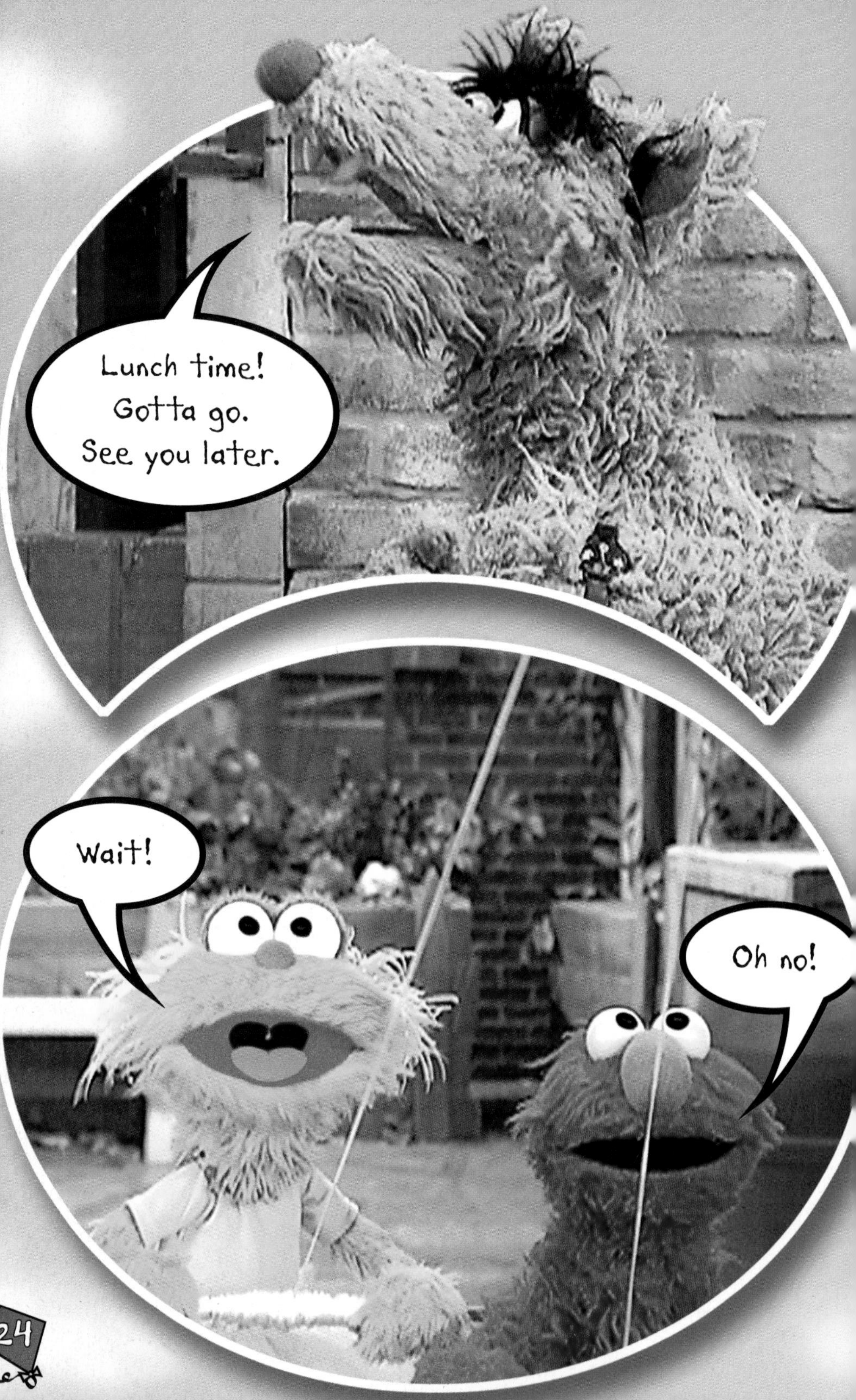
Lunch time! Gotta go. See you later.
Wait!
Oh no!

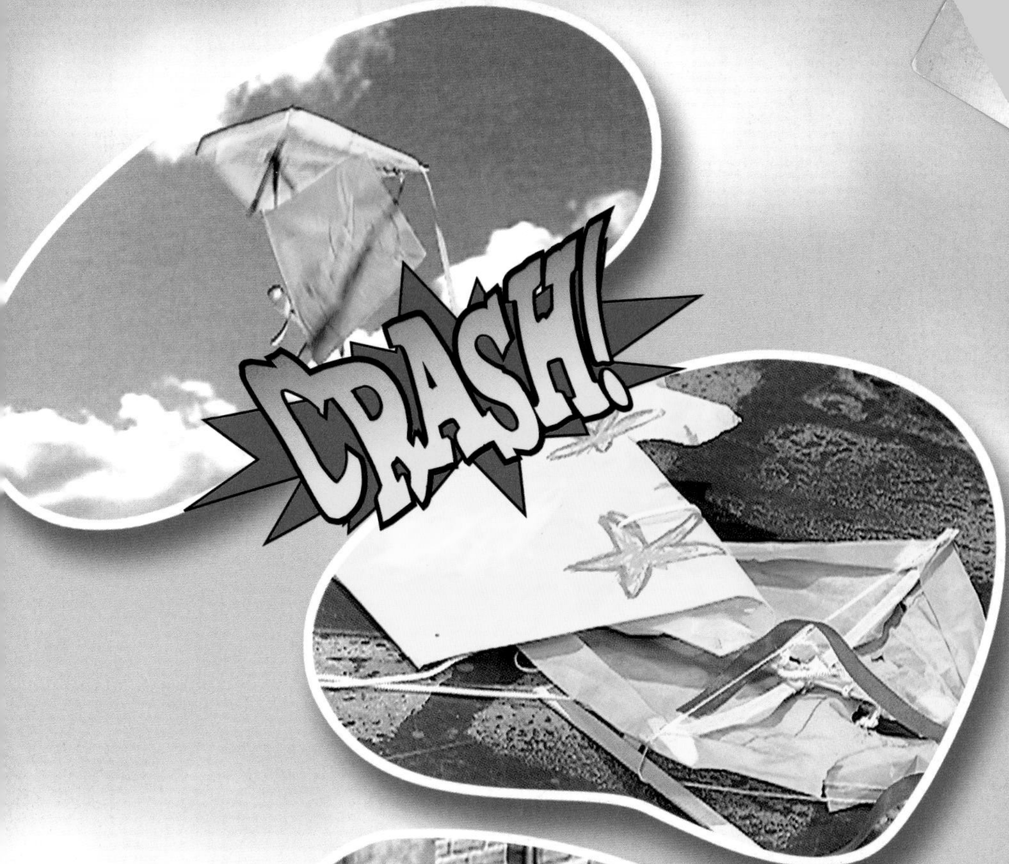
CRASH!

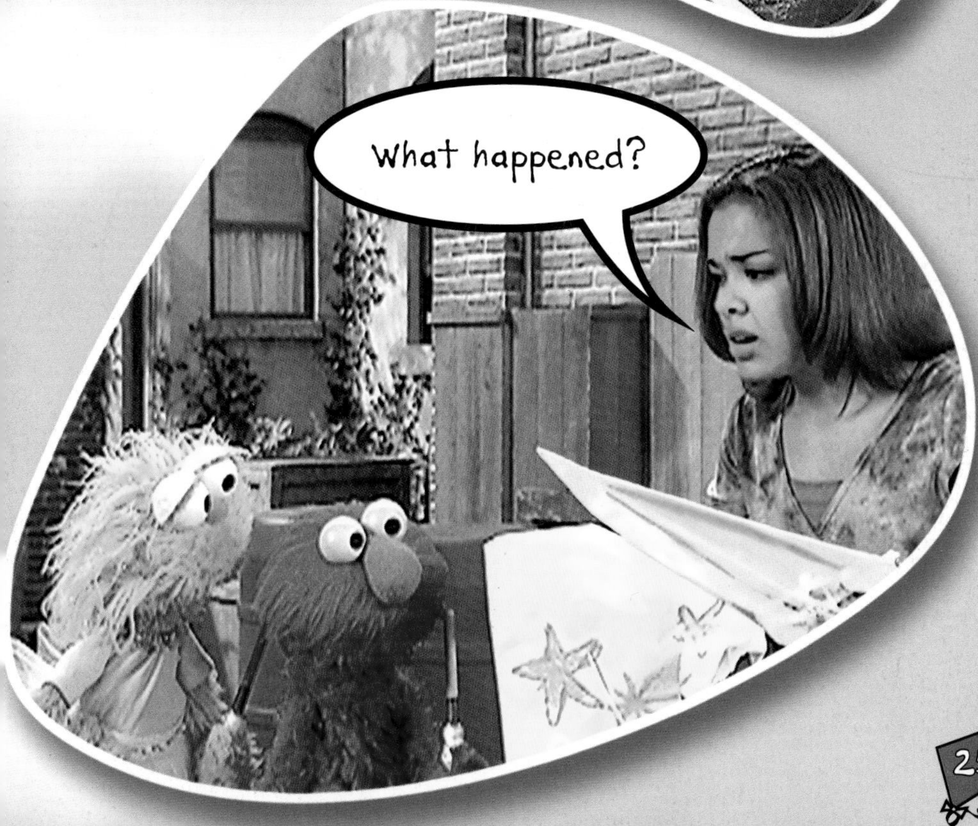
What happened?

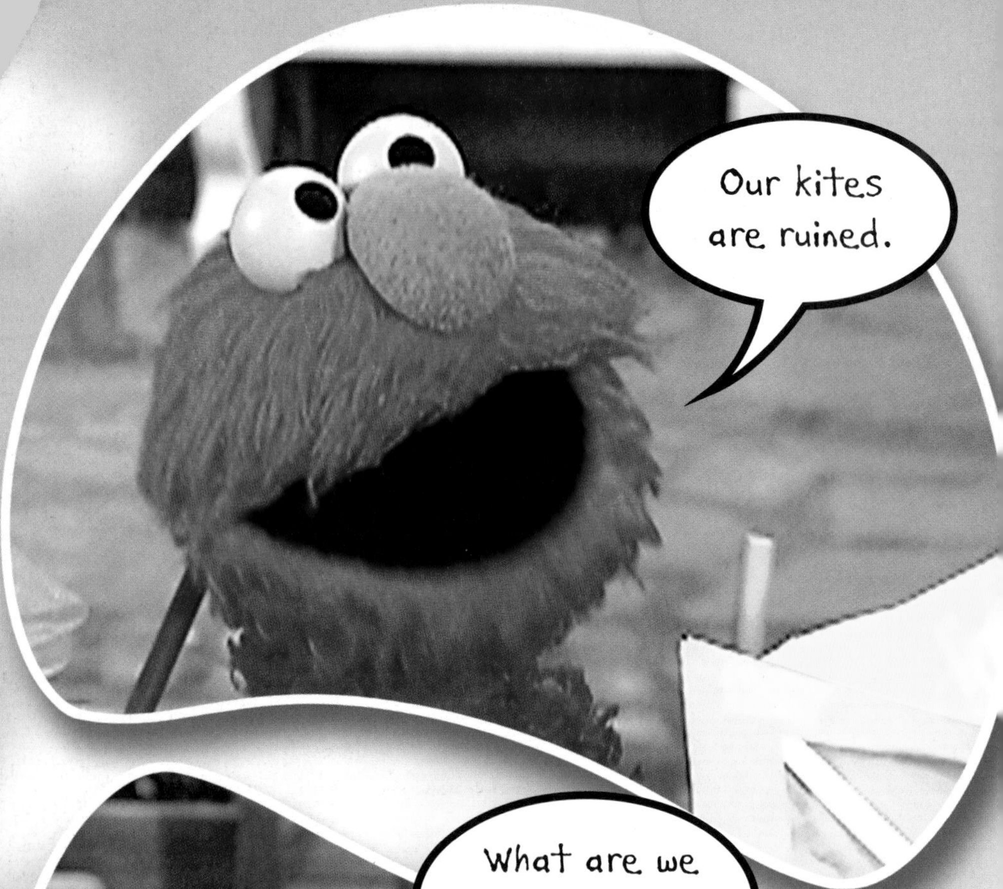
Our kites are ruined.
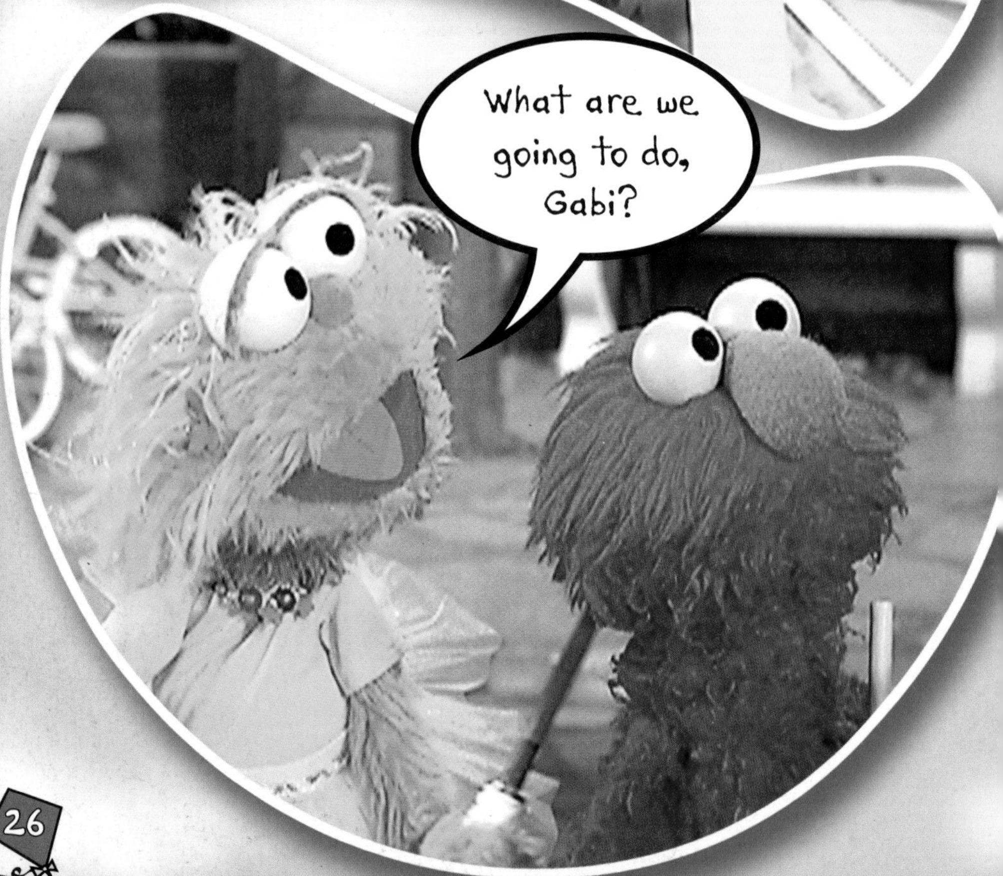
What are we going to do, Gabi?

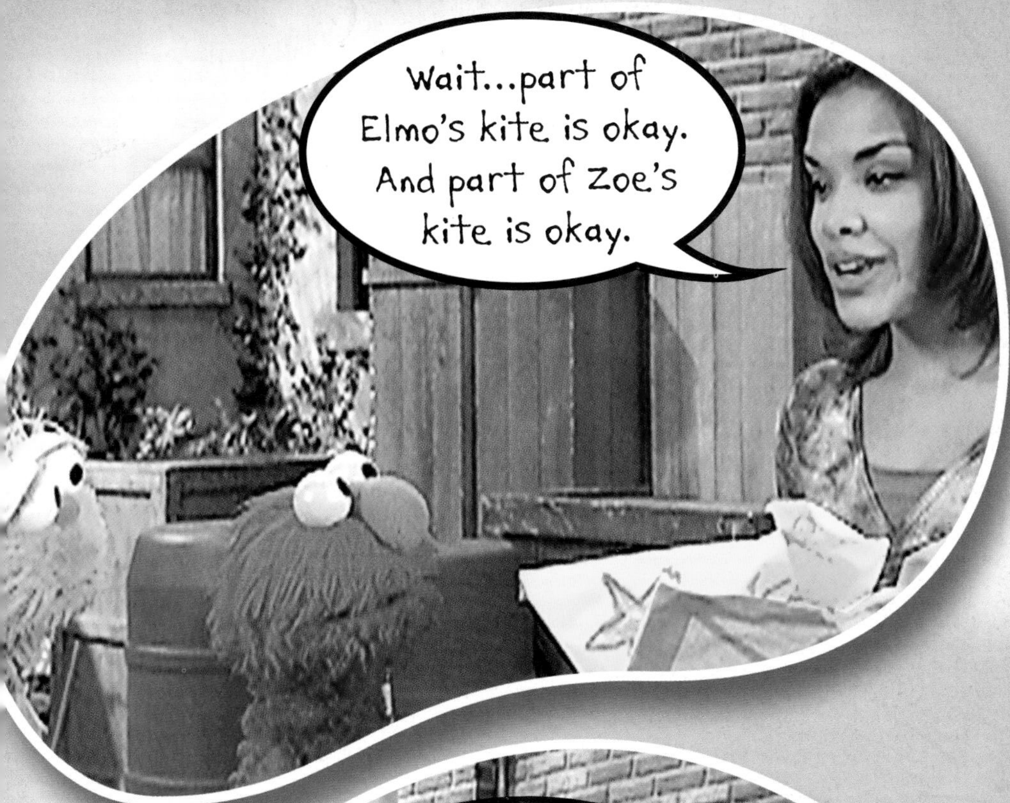
Wait...part of Elmo's kite is okay. And part of Zoe's kite is okay.

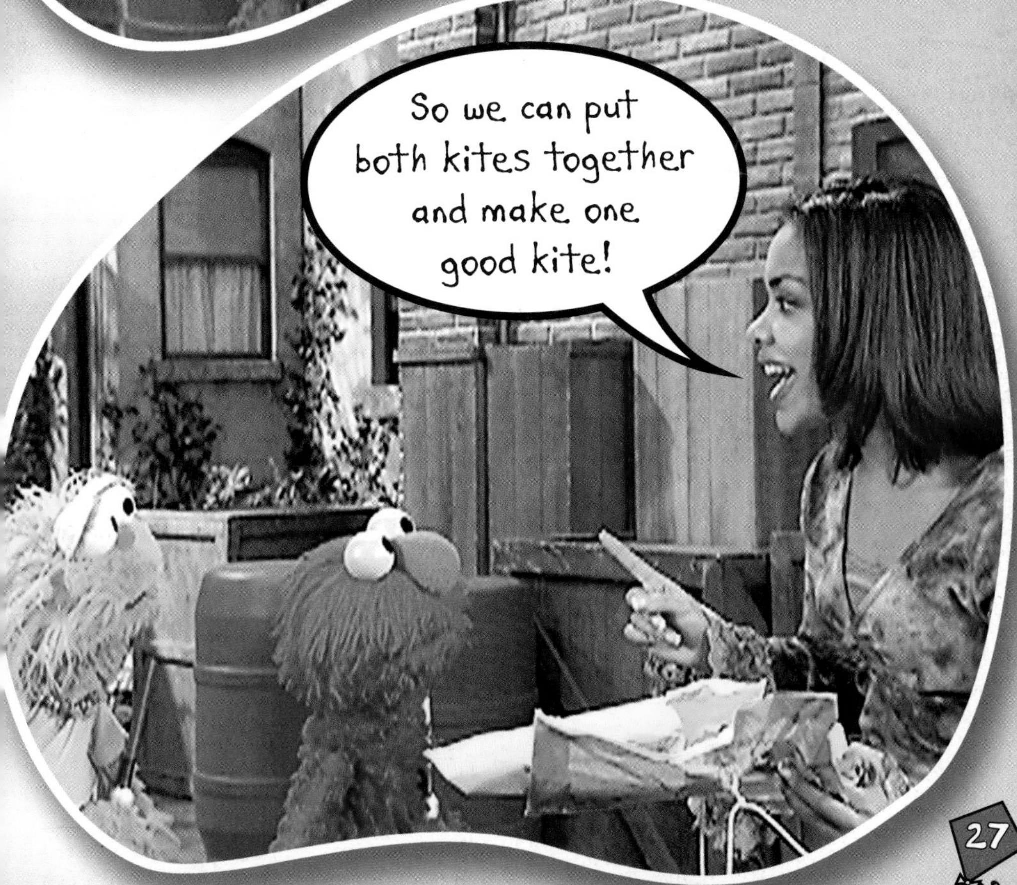
So we can put both kites together and make one good kite!

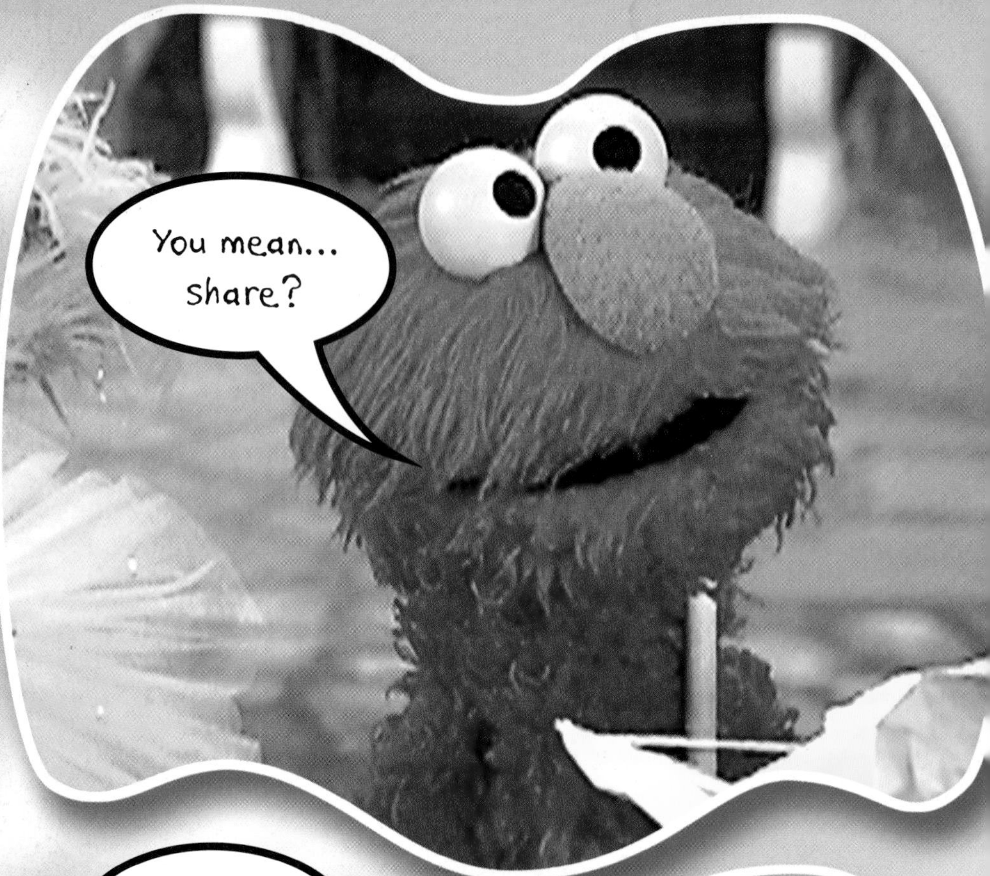
You mean... share?

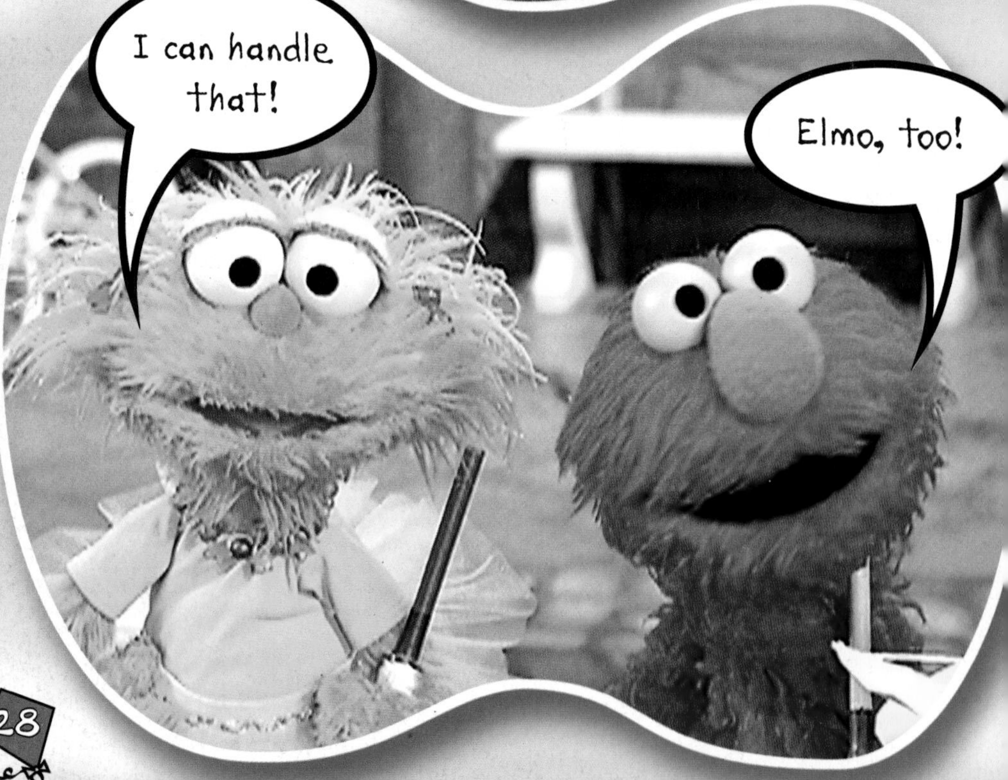
I can handle that!
Elmo, too!

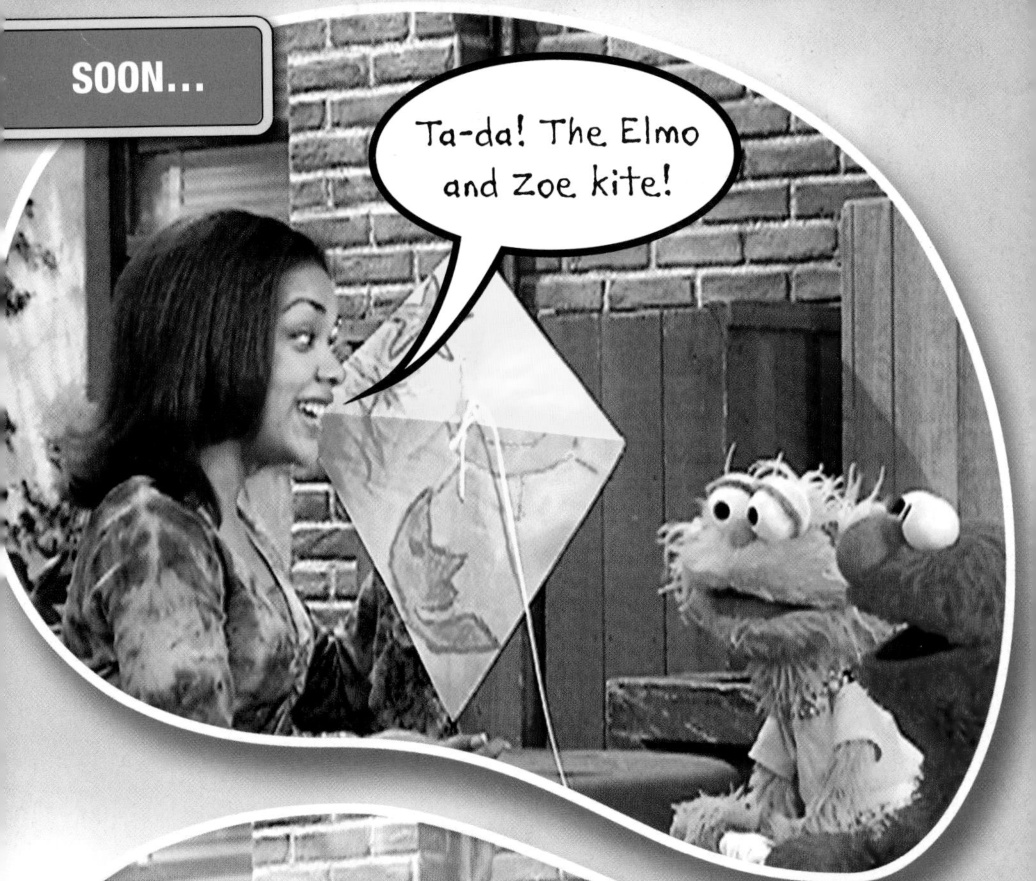
SOON...
Ta-da! The Elmo and Zoe kite!

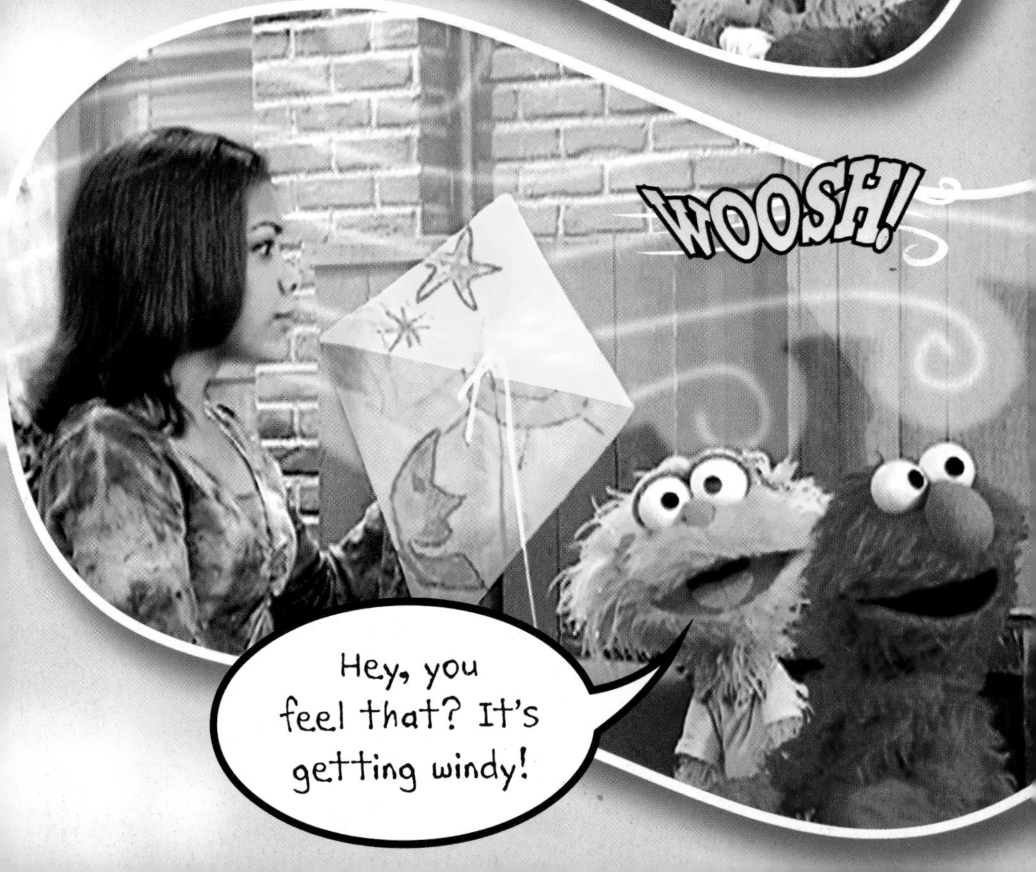
WOOSH!
Hey, you feel that? It's getting windy!

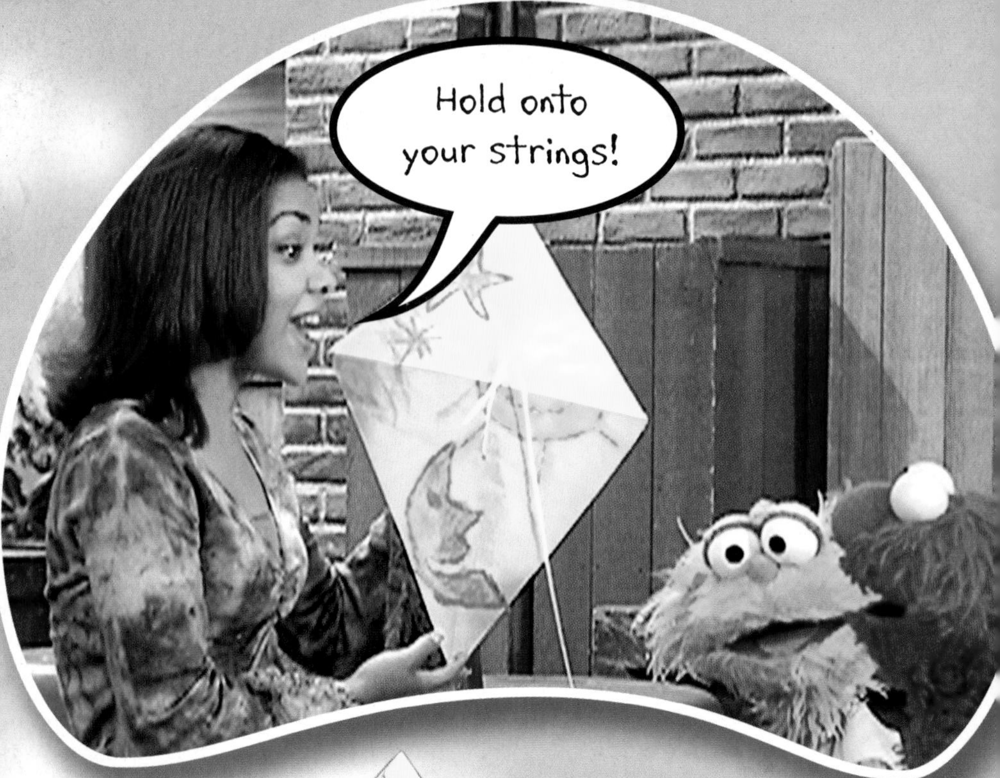
Hold onto your strings!

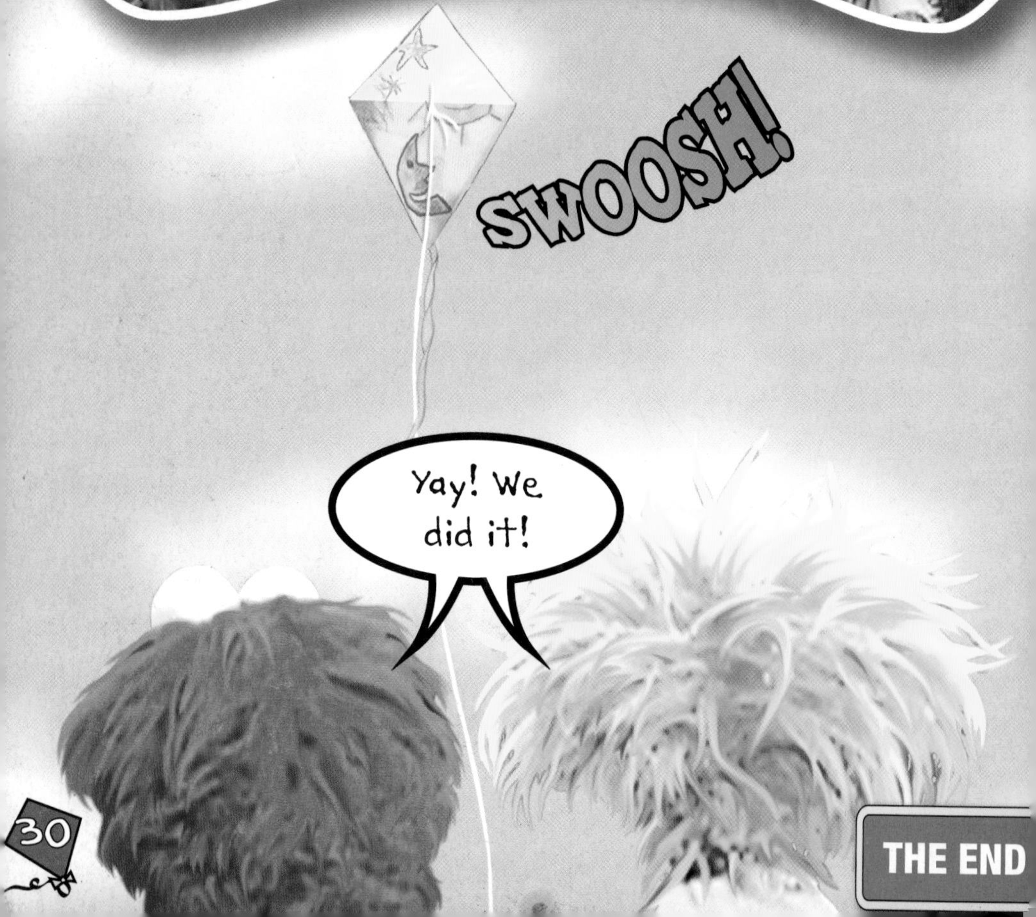
SWOOSH!
Yay! We did it!

THE END

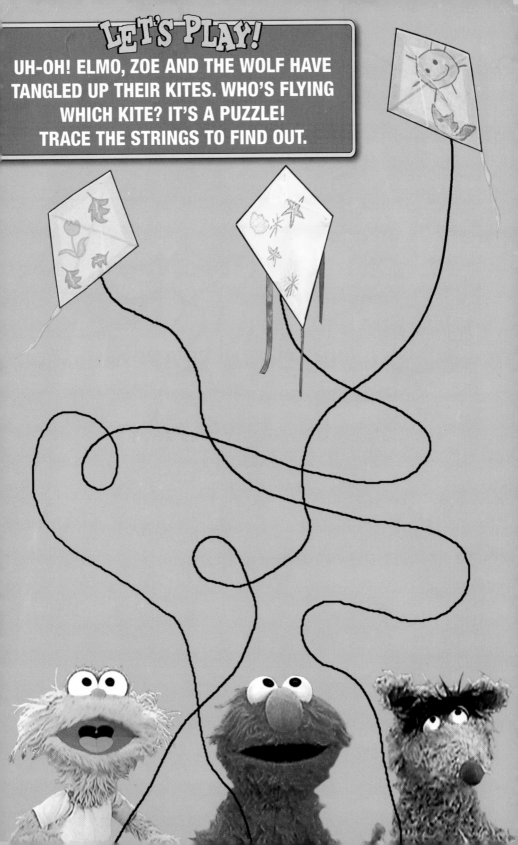

LET'S PLAY!

UH-OH! ELMO, ZOE AND THE WOLF HAVE TANGLED UP THEIR KITES. WHO'S FLYING WHICH KITE? IT'S A PUZZLE! TRACE THE STRINGS TO FIND OUT.